Mandrake the Wild Mallard Duck

To two women in my life
who believed in this book:
My loving and devoted wife, Marilyn,
for her constant encouragement and creative input,
and a very dear friend, Ruth,
who had the faith and conviction to see it in print.

An Oak Hill Books publication.
PO Box 5308
Coeur d'Alene, Idaho
83814
First Edition, September 2000
Printed in USA
Book cover and text ink drawings by the author, Jay David Fisher
Library of Congress Control Number 00-92547

Summary: A flock of "talking" wild mallard ducks fly the long and often hazardous journey late one fall from Canada to the Gulf of Mexico along the Mississippi Flyway. Thirty-two ink drawings visually aid the reader to experience some of the more stressful-and humorous-situations the ducks find themselves in en route. Dramatic, entertaining and educational, and fun to read or listen to.

1. Juvenile literature 2. Young Adult literature 3. Family literature to read to youngsters 4. Senior literature for grandchildren.
ISBN 0-9616701-0-X
10 9 8 7 6 5 4 3 2 1

JAY DAVID FISHER

MANDRAKE the
WILD MALLARD DUCK©

Contents

Illustrations

Introduction

The Mississippi Flyway bordering the Mississippi River is one of the major routes wild ducks, geese and other migratory birds have been flying between Canada and the Gulf of Mexico since time immemorial. No one knows for sure just how long.

Every year in late fall hundreds of thousands of these birds fly south from the Arctic and Canada to escape the cold, harsh winters of the north and enjoy the warm, sunny weather of the rich wetlands and wildlife sanctuaries of the Gulf States. Each spring they return once again to the north, mate, build nests and hatch the next generation of offspring. By fall, most of the newly hatched grow large enough and strong enough to accompany their parents and their flock back once more to the Gulf.

Most wild ducks and geese are gregarious, flying south and north in large flocks. Each species travels with its own kind, that is mallards with mallards, snow geese with snow geese, and so on and so forth. Ducks and geese rarely fly within sight of each other's flock but sometimes frequent the same feeding grounds en route or upon arrival.

Like wild geese, wild ducks fly in a fairly straight V formation whenever they are traveling long distances with one single duck leading the flock at the point of the V. The rest of the flock follows the lead duck in two ever widening rows.

Apparently the lead duck is democratically elected based on attitude, experience and a superior *natural* ability to lead—all essential qualities for a lead duck to most successfully guide a flock of wild ducks to its selected destination. A second "relief" duck is also necessary to spell the lead duck when exhausted, or in the unfortunate event the lead duck meets with an accident or tragedy. The "relief" duck would probably be chosen by the lead duck since they so often work closely together. If the lead duck is lost along the way, the "relief" duck takes over, but only temporarily until another democratic election can be held for a new lead duck.

If all of the above were untrue, argument and confusion would surely ensue—and no one would get anywhere—then none of us would ever witness a beautiful V string of wild ducks flying overhead.

All of this makes a lot of sense, of course—at least to ducks.

The story you are about to read describes the often hazardous, and sometimes humorous, journey one such flock of wild mallard ducks made late one fall from Canada to the Gulf of Mexico along The Mississippi Flyway.

A story that could have happened. And probably did.

Your Author

I
The Arrival

"It's happening Darrell!" Martha shouted excitedly to her husband who was sitting nearby with their three children. "I can feel it . . . and I can hear it! You're about to become a father again, isn't that wonderful!"

Darrell looked up surprised. "Are you sure, Martha?" he asked. "Are you sure you're not just imagining it?"

"Goodness no!" Martha said. "It's for *real* this time—I just know it!"

Her husband was still unconvinced. "Now don't get your hopes up too high, Martha," he cautioned. "You know you've had false alarms before. Maybe this is just another—"

"I know what I know, Darrell!" his wife interrupted firmly. "Just you wait, you'll see!" Martha could feel the movement below her now more than ever, and she was a little upset with her husband's skepticism. But she held such feelings to herself, knowing Darrell would eventually accept what was about to take place, in spite of his caution and doubt.

As the April moon began to illuminate the rim of the Canadian mountains, Martha heard the first crack beneath her warm body. Then—another, louder crack! Cranking her neck, the mallard hen pushed her head beneath her soft down breast, gently nuzzling the single egg that still remained in her nest. Now a light pecking sound came from within the egg and the crack got wider and wider! Thrilled with excitement and anticipation, Martha answered the pecking sound with soft motherly quacking. More pecking and more quacking was exchanged for another minute or two, then suddenly, an oh-so-tiny little yellow bill poked itself out through the widening crack of the shell. Then a tiny wet head peeked out, and shortly thereafter, a tiny little yellowish wet duckling stepped out.

But sadly, the little duckling was not covered all over simply with wet fuzz, as would normally be the case when a duckling is first hatched. Rather, bare spots of skin appeared here and there, making the little duckling look somewhat odd, if not a bit sickly. Too, it's size was much smaller than any of its three siblings, two brothers and a sister, all of whom had been hatched days earlier. Even stranger, the tiny little duckling had very—very—large webbed feet! Way too large for its tiny body! Such misfortune only added to the little duckling's almost humorous appearance.

Loving mother hen that Martha was however, she ignored any such apparent birth defects. Turning to her husband, she clamored excitedly: "You see, Darrell! I just knew our last baby duckling would hatch!"

Darrell was too shocked at the strange looking little duckling to comment. He watched in silence as his wife delicately cleaned off bits of broken shell from the wet little duckling with her bill. Then she cried loudly: "It's a boy, Darrell! We have another boy!"

With his mother's gentle nudging, the little duckling quickly rose to his very large webbed feet, then swung his head about observing the bright new world he had just entered. When he seemed to have his bearings, he instinctively waddled out from the nest, then stood silently before his father with a sheepish smile.

Darrell looked down obviously disappointed. His new son was just too darn small and scrawny even to be a duck, let alone a mallard duck. And no wonder, he told himself, with only three weeks in the shell instead of the normal incubation period of twenty-six days for ducks. Now even more, Darrell questioned why his wife had insisted on laying her fourth egg so late. But he said nothing for he knew the answer to his bewilderment as soon as the thought crossed his mind. Martha simply wanted a larger family.

With the situation beyond his control from the very beginning, Darrell tried to hide his disappointment and regain his composure. "What do you propose to call the little guy, Martha?" he asked weakly. During an earlier conversation the couple had agreed Martha alone would have that choice—if and when her last egg were hatched. The two mallards had named their first three children together, the boys, Darrell Junior and Aaron and their little girl duckling, Jenny.

Martha beamed at her husband's question. "Why we'll call him Mandrake, of course! We'll name him Mandrake II after your father, Mandrake I."

This is not my day, Darrell told himself. Why in the world would she want

DARRELL WAS OBVIOUSLY SOMEWHAT DISAPPOINTED.
THE NEW DUCKLING WAS JUST TOO DARN SMALL AND
TOO SCRAWNY TO BE A MALLARD DUCK!

to name this little peep of a duck after my late father, Mandrake I, the most famous mallard lead duck that ever lived? How could a little duck like this ever hope to follow in such renowned footsteps? And giving him the name Mandrake will only encourage the other ducks to razz him with such a comparison. And for that matter, Darrell continued with himself, why didn't Martha suggest we name one of our first two sons Mandrake? That would have made a lot more sense. Besides, this little guy will probably never even be strong enough to fly south with us in the fall. The Gulf's thousands of miles from here and only the fit and hearty can make that flight.

While all of these questions boggled Darrell's mind, because of his listless nature he refused to discuss such probabilities openly with his wife. Keeping his bill shut was the best way to keep peace in the family, that was Darrell's motto. And peace in the family was all he ever wanted in life. He had no duck dreams nor ambitious goals like his father before him. Leading a flock of wild mallards in and out of one crisis after another was the last thing on Darrell's mind. He would willingly follow the flock and live out his life as an ordinary wild duck—it was that simple.

Martha, of course, was well aware of her husband's feelings toward their new son. She also knew Darrell would never have agreed to the name Mandrake had his opinion been sought. But Martha was a duck with faith and confidence that everything would turn out all right in the end, no matter how trying life might be at times. So she decided to say nothing more to Darrell now. Time alone would help heal her husband's doubts and fears.

When Martha turned her attention to Lil' Manny who had now returned to her nest, Darrell knew it was time for him to leave. Shrugging his shoulders with indifference, he quacked quietly to their other three ducklings, then the four of them waddled off to a nearby lake as Martha continued to clean and nuzzle her new baby son.

The lead duck of Martha and Darrell's flock at the time of this story was a wise old drake named Boris. Boris had been nominated for lead duck by his

THE LEAD DUCK OF MARTHA AND DARRELL'S FLOCK AT
THIS POINT IN TIME WAS A WISE OLD MALLARD DRAKE
NAMED BORIS.

good friend, Mandrake I, whom he had often served with as "relief" lead duck during Mandrake I's fantastic career. Because Mandrake I had also been an excellent teacher in the ways of wild ducks, Boris was easily elected lead duck upon Mandrake I's retirement.

Although Boris had never achieved the level of fame of his predecessor, he was a smart duck, a fair duck and obviously the best duck for the job at the time. Boris was also a brave duck and always put the safety of his flock over himself. Despite his diligence, however, Boris did lose a duck or two on almost every flight, while Mandrake I had made many such flights without the loss of a single duck!

As far as family life, Mandrake I and Boris lead two different lives entirely. As a young drake, Mandrake I found his love quite by accident during a most adventurous circumstance. Then he and his mate quickly flew off together into the morning sun for a life of deep love and respect for each other.

Boris, on the other hand, was not so lucky in love. In fact, he never mated at all so he adopted his entire flock as family once he was elected lead duck. While his interest and understanding of each duck's personal problems had good intention, some said he was too sympathetic. Still, Boris's compassion was respected by most ducks and they followed his lead with little dissention. But that is the way it is with wild ducks. They pick a leader and stick with him—no matter what. It is the law of the ducks.

2
Life's Hardships and Lessons

Spring turned quickly to summer that year in Canada and the transformation among the young ducks of Boris's flock seemed almost magical. Day by day their breasts and wing muscles became stronger and stronger as they practiced flying higher and higher over the trees and around the many lakes. Feathers on the young drakes filled out with glorious plumage and they were soon sporting brilliant emerald-green heads with shiny yellow bills, white neck collars, brown and silver-grey chests and webbed feet as bright as a Florida orange.

The young hens, although more subtle in color than their counterparts, displayed an equally handsome appearance with their rich brown and white feathers, yellow bills and similar orange webbed feet. Both sexes also flashed iridescent blue-and white wing tip bands.

Unfortunately, Lil' Manny, the name every duck called Mandrake except his mother, was developing very, very slowly both in size and a full cover of feathers, much to the silent dismay of Martha. And just as upsetting to Lil' Manny, he was continually razzed by his peers for his diminutive size and funny appearance. Some even referred to him as Dwarfy Duck or Moldy Bird. And he was almost never invited to join in the fun and games of his playmates. This type of rejection and criticism sometimes was more than Lil' Manny could endure. Then he would seek out his mother for comforting. Loving mother that Martha was, she would pull her little son up to her side with a big wing and listen sympathetically to all his woes.

"But, Mom!" Lil' Manny would cry. "All of the little ducks make fun of me, an'...an'...some of the older ducks, too! Just because I'm still small an' don't have all my feathers yet. An' they call me dumb names, too... Dwarfy Duck an' Moldy Bird...an'...an'..."

"Shush now, son," his mother would say softly. "Don't you pay any attention to those who talk like that. You are a smart little duck just like your grandfather Mandrake I was, and one day soon you will grow up big and strong just

"BUT, MOM!" LIL' MANNY WOULD CRY. "ALL OF THE LITTLE DUCKS MAKE FUN OF ME, AN'...AN' SOME OF THE OLDER DUCKS, TOO!"

like all of the other ducks. It will take you a little bit longer, that's all." Then she would hug her son tightly. "Things will get better, son, you'll see." As we already know, Martha had more faith in one little feather than most ducks have on their whole bodies.

Often, after such encouraging talks by his mother, Lil' Manny would waddle away feeling much better and determined to succeed, no matter what anyone else said. Soon he could be seen practicing his flying, flapping along the open ground with all his might or skimming across the tops of lakes until he was finally airborne. For the little duck knew only too well he must build his strength and fly better and better if he were going to be allowed to fly south with the flock in the fall. A final decision that is always made by the lead duck of any flock of wild ducks. In Lil' Manny's case, it was Boris who would decide who goes and who stays behind. Smaller, weaker ducks are often denied the opportunity to accompany the flock because they can slow the progress of the flock and endanger the lives of all of the ducks.

Boris was well aware of Lil' Manny's determination to become one of the flock. He had observed the little duck's drive and respected his courage and stamina. But secretly, Boris was concerned. Still, he wanted to give Lil' Manny every chance to succeed since he knew those who must stay behind usually perish in the cold Canadian winters. Therefore, to inspire and encourage Lil' Manny, Boris spent many extra hours with the little duck that first summer in Canada teaching him all about a wild duck's world. Long after sunset when all of the other ducks were asleep, the big duck and the little duck could be seen sitting quietly on the edge of a lake quacking away to each other. By the end of the summer, the two ducks had become good friends.

During those private conversations, Boris mentioned Lil' Manny's grandfather many times since the two ducks had risked their lives over and over again for the safety of their flock. Of course Lil' Manny wanted to know all about his famous grandfather. While Lil' Manny's mother had talked frequently about Mandrake I to her youngest son, her information as to the secrets of the great duck's success was limited. Boris, of course, had known Mandrake I better than anyone, and was, therefore, the most qualified to explain why Mandrake I had become such a phenomenal success.

So what better role model for Lil' Manny to admire and respect than his own grandfather? After all, both ducks were of the same stock.

"Your grandfather was a very brave and wise duck," Boris told Lil' Manny one evening as the two ducks floated together. "Every duck knew that, of course, but few understood his unique and special talents, most of which I have never seen in any other mallard I have known, quite frankly."

Lil' Manny swam closer to the old drake, curious to know more. "Very special like how?" he asked Boris anxiously. "Please tell me more, Boris, please!"

'Well for starters, your grandfather was a very humble duck. He never bragged about his successes and he let compliments roll off him like water off a duck's back."

Both the big duck and the little duck laughed.

"'And we are all team players,' Mandrake I would say," Boris continued, 'and we must all pull together as a flock helping each other whenever we can.' "This was not always the case, of course," Boris pondered. "Many times your grandfather saved all of us single-handedly with his quick thinking while most ducks were frustrated as to what to do next. He was a true leader in every sense."

"Gosh!" Lil' Manny responded wide-eyed.

"There's more," Boris continued. "Nobody could handle a whole flock or a single duck like Mandrake I. Even if one of the ducks got out of line or became overly selfish your grandfather could put his big webbed foot down faster than you or I could holler 'quack'! But he was also very fair and considerate when necessary."

"Tell me more, Boris, please!"

"Well my boy, I could go on all night. But I do remember one thing in particular that made your grandfather kind of amazing."

"What was that?" Lil' Manny asked excitedly.

"Well . . . it was his unique, almost uncanny ability to navigate us through the most difficult situations, even in the most severe storms . . . and we were through plenty of those. And when it came time for us to land for rest and food, your grandfather always seemed to know the safest place to set down. That's why we made so many successful trips without losing a single duck!" The big mallard stroked the underside of his long bill with a huge wing, contemplating what he had just said. "Perhaps it was only instinct or experience . . . but I prefer to think Mandrake I had a photographic memory as well."

"What's that, Boris? What's a pho-photo-photographic memory?"

"The rare ability some have to record in their minds almost anything they see or choose to remember. Your grandfather had that. He could spot and recognize every town, every highway, forest, lake or river along our flight path to and from the Gulf . . . any crucial landmark that made our trips easier, quicker and safer."

"Gosh!" Lil' Manny exclaimed.

"And because of these unique talents," Boris added, "your grandfather almost always seemed to know where danger lurked. If a duck hunter or any other predator were near, Mandrake I always seemed to know first. Then he would shout for all of us to take off immediately—and in what direction!"

"Boy! My grandfather was really a super duck!" Lil' Manny said.

"Yes he was, my boy," Boris reflected bobbing his dark emerald head, "he truly was an amazing duck . . . simply amazing."

Lil' Manny thanked Boris for describing his grandfather's special talents, then swam off alone to think about it all. Maybe, he thought to himself, he might just have some of those special talents as well. He could already remember most of the local landmarks and lakes, and there was a strong possibility he could predict weather changes, thanks to an earlier discussion with Boris explaining shifting cloud formations with the winds and the colors of the sky. But of course he never told anyone. No one would believe him anyway. "So just maybe my mother is right," he whispered to himself. "Maybe I am a smart little duck after all." With that bit of self-encouragement, the little duck flew one more time around the lakes and over the trees, even though the night was now pitch black.

3
The Adversary & the Admirer

One of the most difficult ducklings Lil' Manny had to contend with that first summer in Canada was a young ruffian named Hector (Hector-the-heckler to many who were intimidated by the mean little duck).

Hector was not only larger than most other ducklings but a bully as well, cracking verbal abuses continually, and sometimes even physically threatening. Because Lil' Manny was the smallest of all the ducklings—and the funniest looking, according to Hector—he was, sadly, picked on the most by Hector.

"Hey, Dwarfy Duck!" Hector would shout sarcastically. "What happened to all of your feathers? Did you get caught in a thrashing machine?" Then he would stick his feathered thumbs into his ears and make weird faces and noises.

Understandably, such rudeness upset Lil' Manny so he never stayed in Hector's presence very long whenever their two paths crossed. A quick exit from the scene was always his safest solution to risk any serious combat. He knew only too well if such a situation did occur, Hector would clobber him.

Such embarrassing confrontations happened frequently between Lil' Manny and Hector, and in time, Lil' Manny began to seriously question whether he really would be big enough and strong enough to join his flock to the Gulf in the fall. Staying behind by himself in the cold Canadian winters would be bad enough-and survival at the best, slim. But knowing his mother would want to stay with him as well would probably mean her sacrifice too! Lil' Manny silently assured himself *that* could not, and would not happen-no matter what!

There was one bright spot in Lil' Manny's life that summer, however, that changed his life forever! The chance meeting of a pretty young girl duckling by the name of Missy Prissy. Lil' Manny had admired her from afar for months. Then, suddenly they met face to face. But as cute as little Missy was, she had a personality flaw that most of her peers disliked. A flaw that was not of her own doing, but it was there.

"HEY DWARFY DUCK!" HECTOR WOULD SHOUT TO LIL' MANNY, "WHAT HAPPENED TO ALL YOUR FEATHERS? DID YOU GET CAUGHT IN A THRASHING MACHINE?"

By an unfortunate tragedy of life, little Missy came into the world alone with no brothers or sisters. Because she was an only child, her mother, Missus Missy Prissy became unconsciously overly protective and cautioned her daughter to be careful of this and careful of that, fearful that little Missy might be hurt or worse, accidentally die. The result of such extreme protection made little Missy feel particularly important, if not superior to her playmates. Soon many of her playmates considered little Missy stuck-up, even spoiled. Some went so far as to say she was spoiled rotten.

But such an unacceptable personality can be easily explained and both mother and daughter forgiven if one considers how this most difficult problem came about.

One dark and cold night the previous April when Missus Missy Prissy was setting on her five eggs nearly ready to hatch, a wild and ferocious raccoon came charging out of the Canadian woods about to attack the helpless mallard hen. In a desperate attempt to protect her eggs Missus Missy Prissy bolted from her nest, faked an injured wing and hopped low across the cold ground with her attacker in hot pursuit. The frightened hen barely escaped with her life when she scrambled into a thicket of thorny brush, just out of reach of the angry raccoon's teeth and sharp claws. Unfortunately, the raccoon did not give up so easily but continued to prance and growl around the thicket until early dawn while Missus Missy Prissy remained trembling inside. Finally, when she felt safe enough to come out of the thicket, she scurried back to her nest of eggs. Sadly, a tragic price was paid when Missus Missy Prissy discovered all her eggs had grown cold—except one—the egg that contained little Missy. All of the rest of her eggs had frozen. Two days later only little Missy hatched.

And that is how little Missy's problem began. She was hatched an only duckling.

Late one fall afternoon while Lil' Manny was sitting alone beneath a tall pine tree little Missy Prissy came waddling by in tears. She had just had another mortifying experience with her playmates and was on her way to find her

MISSUS MISSY PRISSY WAS SETTING ON HER FIVE EGGS WHEN A WILD AND FEROCIOUS RACCOON CAME CHARGING OUT OF THE CANADIAN WOODS . . .

mother for comforting. Because she was confused and her beautiful eyes clouded with tears, she did not see Lil' Manny until he spoke.

"Please don't cry, Missy," Lil' Manny said compassionately. "The other ducks don't mean to be mean to you. They're just scared of anybody who seems a little different. It takes time to grow up and there is so much to learn all the time."

Little Missy stopped dead in her tracks, stunned that even Lil' Manny would speak to her so nicely. She had never really noticed him much before. But now she needed a friend, someone to talk to because her mother was nowhere in sight. As more tears continued to tumble down her pretty face, little Missy tried to explain to Lil' Manny just what had happened. "They—they don't want me to play with them anymore," she sobbed pointing a wing to the other young ducks bobbing and swimming out on the lake. "They said I'm stuck-up an . . . an' spoiled! That's not true, is it Mandrake?"

Lil' Manny was shocked but thrilled that little Missy had called him by his real name. Except for his mother, none of the ducks had ever called him Mandrake, the name he really liked. Finally, someone else was willing to treat him as a normal wild mallard duck—not just some weird feathered thing.

Thrilled with little Missy's friendliness, Lil' Manny pondered her question. He knew from personal experience why she had been treated so unfairly. Now he wanted to give the little hen some hope. "You're not really stuck-up or spoiled, Missy," he said confidently. "You're just a little lonely and frightened because you are growing up alone."

Little Missy was trying hard now to control her tears. She wiped an eye with the tip of one of her beautiful wings. But she needed more assurance. "Do you—do you hate me, too, Mandrake?" she sputtered.

"Of course not!" Lil' Manny replied quickly. "I think you are a very nice duck . . . and a beautiful duck too," he added sheepishly. Now that he had little Missy's undivided attention, he saw his chance to tell her just how much he really liked her.

"That's very sweet, Mandrake," little Missy smiled. "Will you be my friend—please?" She was batting her beautiful wet eyes at him now.

Lil' Manny struggled to hide his excitement. "Sure!" he said. "I'd like that!"

He raised himself up on his big webbed toes, trying to make himself appear taller. It was an unconscious thing. "I know how you feel, Missy. I don't know if you've ever noticed but I've been called names and I just try and forget such words. Our playmates don't really know why they act mean sometimes. They're just scared too. And when we all grow up, we'll see things differently. There'll be more respect for each other, you'll see." Then he thought for a second. "Why, even Hector will probably be a lot nicer," he laughed.

Little Missy giggled at the thought of Hector being nice to anyone. Suddenly she was feeling much better, thanks to Mandrake. Even though the little duck was still missing some feathers and small in stature, in her eyes he had magically become a handsome mallard prince. She looked deep into his flashing black eyes. "Thank you for being so nice to me, Mandrake," she said softly. "You are really a very sweet duck."

For a moment, Lil' Manny was too embarrassed to respond. Everything is too good to be true, he told himself. The girl I've always dreamed of but never dreamed this would happen. Now here she is, standing right before me—and she really likes me. Wow! Finally, he found his voice. "Thank you for calling me Mandrake," he said. "I never did like some of those dumb names I was called sometimes, but I'm still too small to do anything about it, I guess."

"You'll get big," little Missy promised, "just you wait! You'll be as big and as handsome as any mallard drake ever—you'll see! I know you will. Then all of those bad ducks who called you those awful names will be sorry."

While Lil' Manny appreciated little Missy's faith and belief in him, he was not one to begrudge his fellow-duck. Boris had already taught him to understand and be patient with others, even forgiving. Now he saw a chance to help little Missy change her life and become more compassionate to others and live a happier life. He knew she was a good duck deep down inside, just a little confused now, that's all.

Yes, just as his mother had said, Lil' Manny was one smart little duck.

For the rest of that afternoon the two young ducks talked and talked about life and each other, and when darkness began to descend, they had become

LITTLE MISSY STOPPED DEAD IN HER TRACKS, STUNNED THAT EVEN LIL' MANNY WAS SPEAKING TO HER SO NICELY . . . SHE HAD NEVER REALLY NOTICED HIM MUCH BEFORE

good friends. Equally important, little Missy began to understand why she had acted the way she did. And from that day forward, little Missy became a much nicer duck, practicing daily what Mandrake had taught her, particularly the tolerance and forgiveness of others. Soon the other young ducks began to like little Missy—almost to their surprise—and little Missy was not only a beautiful duck outside, but beautiful inside as well.

4
Boris Defends the Weak

"I don't care how hard he's been trying or what his bloodline is!" Ole' Mr. Duckworth snapped one chilly fall morning to Boris. "Lil' Manny is still too small and scrawny to make the flight south with us, and we can't wait any longer. We ought'a be leavin' right now! Besides, even if he can take off with us we'd all be makin' extra stops along the way, not just for Lil' Manny, but some of the other little guys, too! The weak ones will just have to stay behind or the rest of us will be dodge'n shotgun shells when we stop to rest too often."

Boris was patiently waiting for Ole' Mr. Duckworth to finish his speech. The old duck's getting a little crabby and selfish, he thought to himself. But just as he was about to answer Mr. Duckworth, some other ducks, old and young, added their concern.

"Duckworth's got a good point," one said. "It's already mid-October. We should be leaving soon, and if we let Lil' Manny tag along, he'll run out of steam somewhere along the way. Then we'll all suffer!"

A few of the first-timer young ducks almost fully grown by now also stated their objections. "I agree," one replied, "and I for one don't want to end up on somebody's dinner plate because Lil' Manny can't keep up with us!"

"An' why should we all risk our necks for Dwarfy Duck?" Hector quipped. "He's not gonna' make it anyway."

Boris listened stone-faced to those complaining ducks before him. He was well aware the deadline for the flock's departure was drawing near. Few flocks of ducks ever stay in Canada beyond the first or second week of November.

"I DON'T CARE HOW HARD HE'S BEEN TRYING OR WHAT HIS BLOODLINE IS!" OLE MR. DUCKWORTH GRUMBLED. "LIL' MANNY IS JUST TOO SMALL AND TOO SCRAWNY TO FLY SOUTH WITH OUR FLOCK!

But he also knew it was time for him to take a stand on the issue, to set the record straight so to speak. And to remind those ducks who were opposed to the weaker, smaller ducks joining in on the flight south they were losing their love and safety concerns for their fellow-ducks. He resented their selfishness, and told them so.

"Now let's not all get stupid!" he snapped. "First off, none of you younger first-timer ducks know what you're talking about since none of you has ever made the trip yet yourself!

"And frankly, I'm disappointed in some of you older ducks, too!" His bright eyes flashed momentarily at Ole' Mr. Duckworth, then back to the rest of the ducks before him. "You guys have all lived long enough to know little ducks, yes, even small, scrawny little ducks can grow up to be big ducks just like you! You've seen it happen before, little guys becoming winners! So let's all have a little faith in each other and give the little fellows a chance.

"As far as Lil' Manny goes, I believe in him, his mother believes in him . . . and have you seen little Missy with him lately . . . how much confidence and love she has for that little duck? Why I bet that little hen would fly around South America for him if you challenged her. And that's what I call faith! So stop acting so panicky and let's give all the little guys a little more time to fully develop. We've still got some time left before we absolutely have to leave." Boris paused for a moment to see if any of his lecture was getting through and to wait for any rebuttal. When there was none, he continued.

"Just remember who you elected as your lead duck," he said. "My decisions are final—you all know that! So Lil' Manny and any other smaller ducks who can take off with us are going and I want all of you to support them—willingly!" Boris flashed a glance once more at Ole' Mr. Duckworth. "As for you fellows who started this ruckus, I'm going to forget I ever heard it. The matter is closed!" Then the big mallard drake turned and waddled away.

When Boris left the ducks he went off to search for Martha to express his concern not only for Lil' Manny's dubious ability to make the Gulf but his own decision to continue to delay the flock's departure date. Was he really risking the lives of everyone just to give Lil' Manny more time to develop? Would there really be too many emergency landings in unfamiliar territory? Could Lil' Manny, the smallest of all the little first-timers even keep up if he were allowed to go? All of these questions staggered Boris's mind as he found Martha standing quietly alone at the edge of a small lake.

"Martha," he began softly. "The winds are changing and the skies growing darker almost daily. So you know that means all of us will be heading south soon, hopefully before any major storm hits." He paused, looking soberly into the mallard hen's eyes, then raised the fateful question. "Do you think Lil' Manny will be ready when it is time to go?" he asked.

Martha shifted nervously. She had been dreading this question for weeks every time she looked at her small son. But she knew she had to offer Boris some hope. "He has the burning desire," she remarked slowly. "And as you know, Boris, he has been practicing his flying hard all summer. I hope and pray he's ready to go soon and I pray even more he can make it all the way . . . but I can't be sure." She paused briefly, looking at Boris with uneasiness, then continued. "But please give him a chance, Boris," she pleaded. "It can't be too risky for others if we make just a few extra stops where you know it is safe, can it?" She waited for his response.

"Martha," Boris said calmly gazing into her eyes. "I've known you and your family for several years now, and we both remember how strong and brave Lil' Manny's grandfather was. There isn't a duck along the Mississippi Flyway who hasn't heard of the magnificent feats of Mandrake I. He was the best there ever was!" The wise old mallard hesitated, then went on. "But Martha, we both know *that* kind of background, heritage, those powerful genes, are seldom passed on to later generations—at least to any similar degree. Even though we both know Lil' Manny dreams of being that kind of super courageous duck one day.

"But my dear, let us both be realistic and honest with each other, as I trust we always have been. Duck dreams are okay, but Lil' Manny's case is different. He's starting from way behind . . . and I mean *way* behind! And right now, I can't tell you if he'll be ready or not though he's looking stronger every day. But as far as making it all the way to the Gulf with us, who knows? Nobody!"

"I understand," Martha returned unflinchingly.

"I hope you do, Martha. I think you know I love the little guy, too. He's like the son I never had. That's why I've spent any extra time I had this summer to teach him all about a wild duck's challenges. And I can tell you one thing for sure, he's one smart little duck, he's a fast learner . . . and not incidentally, he has a great heart, too!"

"Thank you for those comforting words, Boris," Martha said. "That means a lot to me."

"Well, it's easy to tell the truth, Martha. But may I remind you, my dear, all of these fine duck qualities tell us nothing about his physical stamina. You and I know flying thousands of miles for the first time is a real test for any young duck."

The mallard hen remained silent, awaiting her lead duck's final decision.

"But I promise you right here and now, Martha," Boris said straightforwardly, "When we take off soon, Lil' Manny will be on the flight line with us. I'll see to that! I'm still the lead duck of this flock by majority vote and all of my decisions are final. Every single duck in our flock knows that!

"Not incidentally," Boris continued, "I've already had a few complainers, not only about Lil' Manny going along but some of the other first-timer ducks, too, but I just straightened out those ducks a few minutes ago."

"I'm very grateful to you, Boris."

"Don't thank me yet, Martha," Boris retorted. "I haven't finished. Now here comes the tough part. If Lil' Manny, or any other weaker duck for that matter, needs too long to rest and recuperate along the way, if I feel at anytime the flock as a whole is endangered beyond any normal risk landings, we will all take off immediately—with or without that weaker duck!"

Martha stood tall and straight without comment, accepting her lead duck's pronouncement with dignity and respect.

Boris concluded. "And of course if one of those little ducks happens to be Lil' Manny, heaven forbid, and if you choose to stay behind with him, and I know you would, I'll understand."

"Of course," Martha answered solemnly.

"Well perhaps under those dire circumstances, Darrell would stay with you too. But I also realize you have three other children to worry about, so that decision would be yours and Darrell's . . . should it ever arise. Meanwhile, Martha, you know my job is to look out for the flock as a whole over any single duck's life, tough as that kind of decision can be sometimes."

"I understand," Martha said. "I just want you to know, Boris, I'm very grateful to you for all you have done to help Mandrake this past summer. He, too, is very appreciative, I know. He really respects you a lot. You are a wise and wonderful friend, Boris, and I know the flock comes first in any crisis." Martha's eyes took on a misty look. "If Mandrake does falter along the way, yes, I will stay with him, regardless of the consequences. Darrell, on the other hand, I would insist fly on with the children. They still need his protection on such a long flight."

Boris looked hard into Martha's gentle eyes.

"Martha, you are truly one fine lady duck!" he said. "It is a pleasure to know you. I only hope and pray none of our bad thoughts here today come to pass and that we all arrive safely in the Gulf. I shall do my utmost to get us there."

"Thank you, Boris," Martha said softly. "Thank you for everything."

"You are very welcome, indeed!" Boris returned. Then the big drake cocked his shiny green head and pondered the graying sky in silence for a moment. "We'll be leaving in two or three weeks, Martha. I'll let you know." Then he turned and waddled away.

As Martha looked after Boris a lone tear began to puddle in one eye. She quickly wiped it away with the tip of her feathered wing.

5
The Long Flight Begins

Strong November winds saw the cold sweep down from the far north, completing the task of cleaning off the few rust and gold leaves from the trees. Winter was about to descend on Canada.

Boris could wait no longer. At dusk he gathered all of his flock around the edge of a large lake and from higher ground, announced an early morning departure for the following day with Harold as his personal choice for second-in-command, the "relief" lead duck, as it were.

The flock's itinerary would be the same as last year and every year before that. South from Canada across the northeast corner of North Dakota to Minnesota, then down the Mississippi Flyway along the Mississippi River to the Gulf of Mexico. Their final destination would be the Bonnet Carre Wildlife Management Area on Lake Pontchartrain, just outside of New Orleans, Louisiana.

"Oh, one more thing!" Boris reminded himself. "Before we break up here, I would like to announce that this will be my last flight as your lead duck."

A moaning, "Oh, no!" swept over the flock. Boris was popular despite his unusually long delay this time leaving Canada.

"Yes, I mean it!" Boris repeated loud and clear. "This is my last lead. I'm getting too old and tired. I'll step down and fly off the wing of your new lead duck when we all return next spring. So start thinking seriously about my replacement, and remember, you all know the rules. Nominate whomever you like and a two-thirds majority wins. I want a new lead duck picked *before* we head back."

Boris paused briefly studying his flock, then, "Okay, that's about it. Any questions? When there were none, he concluded. "Then Harold and I will meet you all right here just before sunrise . . . and good luck to all of us."

Lil' Manny flew near the back of the flock with his mother. His brothers, Darrell Junior and Aaron and his sister, Jenny flew farther up the V formation with their father, Darrell. Missy, who was now completely devoted to Lil' Manny and very concerned about his physical ability to make the long flight, flew just behind the little duck and off his right wing. Even though Lil' Manny had matured almost to a normal drake size he was still missing feathers, and she wanted to monitor his condition regularly. Should he suddenly become too weak to continue, she would stay with him while Martha flew ahead to tell Boris. Hopefully, the flock would then land for rest and food.

Missy's mother, Missus Missy Prissy, also flew near the back of the flock where she could offer moral support to her daughter and Lil Manny. She had encouraged their affection for each other from the beginning and was an intelligent and sympathetic mallard hen.

For the first day of flying Lil' Manny did just fine, holding his own with the rest of the flock during several landings for rest and feeding. While some of the ducks were surprised at Lil' Manny's stamina, Lil' Manny was not. After all, he had practiced flying harder and longer in Canada than any of the other young ducklings. Now he was determined to fool them all—young and old alike.

But after two days en route just before the Canadian-U.S. Border when the flock landed once again, Lil' Manny began to show signs of tiring. Boris came over to check on his condition for a first-hand report from Martha and Missy. Both mallard hens were anxiously concerned, but when Lil' Manny said he was fine, Boris took him at his word. After a brief pep talk by the duck leader, the flock took off once more.

The next day, however, Lil' Manny was having serious trouble keeping up and began to slowly drift back from the flock. Martha and Missy fell back with him for encouragement.

"Keep flying, son!" his mother cried. "We must be over Minnesota now and I'm sure Boris will have us land soon."

BORIS COULD WAIT NO LONGER. AT DUSK THE NEXT EVENING HE GATH-
ERED ALL OF HIS FLOCK AROUND AND ANNOUNCED AN EARLY MORNING
DEPARTURE.

Lil' Manny looked at his mother but did not speak. He needed all his strength just to keep flying. Martha and Missy were alarmed. "Martha, can't we do something for him?" Missy pleaded. "I know he's getting very tired. He's got to rest again."

Martha agreed. Picking up speed she flew to the front of the flock to talk with Boris. Immediately he signaled the flock to land at a lake directly below. Then he guided everyone out to the middle of the lake to avoid sheets of ice forming along a shoreline already crusted with snow from a recent storm. With temperatures dropping, Boris knew the best feeding was on open water where the flock could skim nourishment from floating seeds and insects. Rooting for vegetables and seeds on frozen ground would be next to impossible.

Totally and completely exhausted Lil' Manny landed on a frozen snow bank hundreds of yards from his flock out on the lake. He was lucky to get down at all without just falling right out of the sky. He was that bushed. And when he thought about the hundreds and hundreds of miles that still lay ahead to the Gulf, his future looked very dim, indeed.

But Lil' Manny was not alone for long. Terribly concerned, Martha and Missy soon came swimming up, then joined him on the frozen turf.

"We were wondering what happened to you, son," Martha said, trying hard not to notice how exhausted Mandrake looked.

"Are you okay?" Missy asked compassionately.

"I'm kind of beat, Missy," Lil' Manny confessed, now steadying himself with both wings stretched to the frozen ground. "I just don't seem to have enough lift anymore."

The two mallard hens looked at him with fear and doubt.

Lil' Manny tried to lift their spirits. "But I think I'll be okay . . . if I can just rest awhile."

Then Boris dropped in from the sky. "How's it going, my boy?" he asked. "Is there anything we can do for you?" Boris knew there was a serious problem unfolding this time.

Lil' Manny sensed his anxiety. He knew he had to convince all three mallards he would carry on. Through hard puffing breaths he said, "I'm ready when you are, sir. Just say the word." He tried to chuckle.

While Boris was impressed with Lil' Manny's perky attitude, he knew the little duck was faking. Yet because of the obvious deep concern Martha and Missy displayed, he did not yet have the heart to leave Lil' Manny behind.

"I think we'll all spend the night here," Boris said studying the position of the cold winter sun. "Even though it's only about three, we can all feed up now before dark. Then we'll head down south early in the morning."

The mallard hens knew Boris was favoring Mandrake but neither was about to concede the truth. Missy changed the subject.

"Are we anywhere near the Mississippi River yet, Boris," she asked casually.

"It's only about a hundred miles that way," the big drake said pointing with his large wing. "Probably should reach it early tomorrow morning, I should think." He looked at Lil' Manny. "Son, I want you to get out there on the lake with the rest of us and chow down. You need energy. I want to see you bright-eyed and bushy-tailed in the morning, all right?"

"Yes, sir!" Lil' Manny said. "In just a few minutes."

"Missy and I will go with him," Martha said, "but is it okay if the three of us rest up here a bit first?" she asked.

Boris looked about. "Well," he said slowly, "I guess you'll be safe. We're pretty far from any farms. I studied the territory as we were landing. But we still have to watch out for hunters and dogs," he warned. "Especially when we take off at dawn. That's when they do all of their serious hunting."

"We'll be careful," Martha promised. "And thank you for landing us."

"I think the whole flock was a little exhausted this time," Boris said, "so I'm not really favoring just Lil' Manny. Besides, we all need food, too."

Rest and food for a tired flock was true. But stopping as early as three O'clock in the afternoon could have been debated by more ambitious lead ducks.

"We'll see you all later," Boris said. Then he flew off to join the rest of the flock out on the lake.

Lil' Manny's father, Darrell, came by a few minutes later. But his lack of concern for his son's welfare was disappointing to Martha. Darrell seemed more upset with 'all of the delays' than whether or not his little son could continue on.

Martha responded with a "shush" and chased him off.

Lil' Manny's older brothers, Junior and Aaron, were also uninterested in their baby brother's future. They were too busy frolicking out on the lake with the other young ducks.

But Lil' Manny's sister, Jenny, was becoming much more compassionate, now that she had matured into a young mallard hen. Soon she came swimming up to the shoreline, then joined everyone on the frozen snow.

"How are you feeling, little brother," she asked. "Golly, I'll bet you're tired. I know I am. I had no idea flying this far was so hard, did you?"

"I'm okay, Jenny," Lil' Manny said, still propping himself up with his wings to the frozen ground, "but thanks for your concern."

Jenny looked out at her two brothers on the lake. "Just look at them, Mother," she said, "bobbing and swimming around like they haven't a care in the world. Don't they really care about Lil' Manny?"

"Junior and Aaron are young mallard drakes, Jenny," Martha said. "They aren't concerned about families yet, until they have their own. We just have to accept that."

"Well, it certainly doesn't seem right to me," Jenny retorted.

Lil' Manny was getting upset with all of the attention on himself. "Don't you worry about me," he said shifting his wings to imply he was now moving freely. "In the morning I'll be ready to take off with the rest of . . ."

"Shush!" Missy whispered, interrupting Lil' Manny. "Did you hear that?" The young hen stared hard at some tall reeds at the edge of the icy bank.

All of the mallards focused on the tall reeds.

"There's something in there," Missy said softly. "I know it—I know it for sure!"

Everyone watched intently toward the reeds, they waited, and they listened . . .

6

Everett, the Snow Goose

The crackling sound in the frozen reeds continued to get louder and louder.

"Can anybody see anything in there?" Jenny blurted out.

"I can't see anything," Missy whispered, "but I know there's something in there!"

"Be still!" Lil' Manny commanded—"all of you! If I say *fly,* fly out of here as fast as your wings will carry you—and over the water! It's our best chance if a dog or hunter is in there."

"Mandrake's right, girls," Martha said. "Do what he says." The mallard hen was terribly proud of her young son at that moment. As exhausted as he was, he instinctively took control of what could be a serious situation.

Now another rustling sound came from the tall reeds, but it was much louder and much closer. All four mallards were poised to take off when suddenly the reeds parted and out waddled a very tall, sooty looking young white snow goose. He had very large yellow webbed feet, a rather oddly shaped grey bill and black-tipped wings.

"Hi, folks!" the young snow goose said gayly. "Mind if I join you?"

"Who—who are you?" Lil' Manny asked.

"My name is 'Everett,'" the snow goose said as he slowly approached the mallards. Then one of his huge yellow webbed feet trampled the other and he almost fell over. "Woops!" he grinned. "Guess my feet are kinda big, but they sure are great for snow." Recovering, he stood up straight and tall.

SUDDENLY, THE REEDS PARTED AND OUT WADDLED A VERY TALL, SOOTY LOOKING YOUNG WHITE SNOW GOOSE . . .

"Where did you come from?" Lil' Manny asked.

"From right over there," Everett said confidently pointing back to the reeds with a huge wing.

"I know that," Lil' Manny said a bit annoyed. Then he sensed the snow goose might just be a little slow and asked more pleasantly, "I mean where did you come from before you got here?"

"Ohhhhh, you mean where is my home, right? Well, sir, I'm from way up in Can-e-da, way, way up in Can-e-da!" The snow goose knew he had already flown a great distance.

"And where is the rest of your flock, young man . . . and your parents?" Martha asked.

"Well, mam," Everett said blinking sadly, "I—I lost my father and my mother a few stops back . . . hunters." The snow goose sniffled slightly but fought back tears.

"Oh, how terrible," Martha said. "You poor dear."

"That's awful!" Missy added. "Then where is your flock?"

"I—I don't really know," the goose said scratching the top of his head with a wing. "It's difficult for me to believe sometimes, but I do believe they took off without me. They did once before but I flew like crazy and caught up with them again."

"How selfish," Jenny said.

"Well I'm sure there is a logical explanation, Everett," Martha said consolingly, even though she knew wild geese seldom show any patience or affection for orphan goslings. But she wanted to give the snow goose some hope. She turned to the mallards. "Did any of you see a flock of snow geese as we flew in?"

Everyone answered, "NO!"

"They're probably looking for you somewhere right now, Everett," Martha said, "so you just stay right here with us until they find you, okay?"

"Well thank you, mam!" Everett said bobbing his head in gratitude. "I really appreciate your hospitality, I truly do, yes, mam." In spite of his slowness, Everett had a way with words that touched the heart. Everyone was impressed.

As Lil' Manny listened, he was already forming a plan to rescue the lone goose. "I'll speak to our lead duck, Boris," he said. "I'm sure he'll let you fly on with us to the Gulf, Everett, if we don't find your flock first." He knew the goose needed the protection of other birds on such a long flight ahead. It would be too dangerous for such a young goose to fly all that way alone.

"That is very kind and considerate of you . . . you . . . ah, what are your names, may I ask? We're chatting here and I don't know who any of you nice folks are."

"I'm sorry, Everett! It's my fault," Lil' Manny said. He turned to his companions. "This is my mother, Martha, my sister Jenny and my girl friend, Missy . . . and I'm Lil' Manny."

"MANDRAKE NOW" Martha and Missy said loudly in unison.

"I'm very pleased to make all of your acquaintances, I'm sure," Everett said bobbing his head to each as they were introduced. "You are all very kind and sympathetic ducks." Then he reflected a bit. "My mother was like that. She used to say 'If birds of a feather don't stick together they'll stick in somebody's pan.'" Then he laughed.

"Your mother was right," Martha said. "God Bless her for teaching you to be kind and understanding of others. Life gets very difficult at times and that is when we do need to stick together." Leaving a fine young strapping snow goose alone to die like this was a chilling thought, Martha reflected. She looked at Mandrake but hid her fears with a question. "Are you hungry yet, son?"

"I still need a little more rest, Mother," Mandrake answered. "Then I'll join you all out on the lake—I promise!" He shifted his body slightly but continued to support himself with his wings stretched again to the frozen turf. That was when Everett first noticed Mandrake was missing some feathers and appeared very tired. The goose just never noticed things like that until someone pointed them out. But when they did, he was always very concerned for their welfare.

"I'll stay with him, mam," Everett volunteered happily.

"You don't have to do that," Lil' Manny said.

"But I *want* to!" the snow goose insisted.

"That's a nice gesture, indeed," Martha said. "Thinking of others first. It makes the girls and me feel much better knowing you are here to keep my son company. He's very tired from the long flight and as you can see, he hasn't quite filled out with all his feathers yet."

"Don't you worry, folks," Everett said. "Me and Mandrake will be just fine. Now you ladies do have a good feed, won't you. We'll join you soon."

"Thank you, Everett," Martha said. "You are a very sweet young goose. Come girls, let's go." With Lil' Manny and Everett remaining on shore, the three mallard hens entered the water.

While Lil' Manny and Everett sat together on the frozen turf getting better acquainted, Lil' Manny filled the snow goose in on his life's story to date. He concluded by confiding in Everett that he did not think he had the strength to go on much farther, let alone ever reach the Gulf.

"And if I do stay behind," Lil' Manny said, "I'd be grateful, Everett, if you would look after my mother and my sister and Missy until they reach the Gulf."

Everett appreciated Mandrake's confidence in him already, but he would not agree with the little duck's negative conclusion. "That is not going to happen to you, my friend," the snow goose said most assuredly. "You simply need some rest and some food for energy. You'll be okay soon, when . . ."

Just then another young mallard drake came out of the same frozen reeds from where Everett had appeared. He waddled toward them. Unfortunately, it was Hector!

"Well, well, well," he said sarcastically. "The one and only Dwarfy D—" He stopped short, glaring at the big white snow goose. "Wait a minute! What have we here? A snow baboon, perhaps? Or could this be the original Silly Goose?"

"We don't need your company, Hector," Lil' Manny said. "We're doing just fine."

"Well you don't look fine to me," Hector returned. "And a lot of young drakes in our flock are taking bets you don't ever make the Gulf—so there!"

Everett was getting upset fast. This was one mean duck. "I don't know who you are, sir, but I do believe you should show more respect for your fellow-duck."

Hector looked hard at the snow goose. "And where did you come from, ice monster, the moon? Does the government know there's an alien loose on this planet?"

Lil' Manny had had enough. "Don't pick on my new friend," Hector," he scolded. "He's a nice snow goose and he's already flown farther than you or I. Everett is from way up in Canada."

"I doubt if he flew here," Hector jibbed. "He probably took a bus. And by the looks of him, I think he missed a few connections!" Hector was laughing so hard now his sides ached.

"You better not push your luck, Hector," Lil' Manny warned. "Everett is a lot bigger than you."

"C'MON, YAH BID DUMB GOOSE!" HECTOR
JEERED—HE RAISED HIS FEATHERED
FISTS, THEN BEGAN DANCING AROUND
EVERETT. "PUT'EM UP, YOU STUDID CLUTZ!"
HE SHOUTED.

"Bigger maybe, but no match for Hector-the-wrecker!" The mean duck
raised his feathered fists and began to dance around Everett. "C'mon, yah big
dumb goose! Put'em up, you stupid clutz!"

The gentle goose stepped back. "I have no quarrel with you, duck . . . and I
don't want to hurt you."

"HA! You couldn't hurt a water bug!" Hector cried.

"Leave Everett alone!" Lil' Manny warned again.

"Stay out of this, Dwarfy Duck!" Hector demanded, shoving Lil' Manny
down hard on the frozen ground as he continued to circle the snow goose.

As Lil' Manny struggled to his feet, Hector shot out his first blow at Everett.
The snow goose easily avoided the punch by stepping back casually on one
huge webbed foot, keeping the other firmly planted. The swing barely clipped
the tip of Everett's oddly shaped bill.

Lil' Manny shouted, "Stop it, Hector!" But the mean duck ignored him.

Then another feathered-fist shot out, this time finding its mark dead center! But the punch was *not* thrown by Hector but by the snow goose. And it

caught Hector squarely in the face, knocking him silly instantly—much to Everett's surprise.

"I warned you, duck . . . and I'm really sorry!" Everett said apologetically. He turned to Lil' Manny. "Do you think I hit him too hard? I just meant to scare him when I swung but he walked right into me. Aren't ducks suppose to duck?"

"Don't worry about it, Everett," Lil' Manny grinned. "He's out cold now but I'm sure he'll wake up soon. He's had a punch like that coming for a long time from somebody. Now let's go take our swim. I'm hungry now." As Lil' Manny and the snow goose swam out from the shore, Lil' Manny looked back to see Hector already on his feet, shaky, but standing. "You see!" Lil' Manny said. "He's already recovered!"

"Oh, good!" Everett said happily. "Now I feel better."

Lil' Manny felt better too. Not because Hector had finally been taught a lesson, but because he had met a good new friend in Everett, the snow goose.

BUT THIS TIME THE PUNCH WAS THROWN BY THE SNOW GOOSE AND IT CAUGHT HECTOR SQUARELY IN THE FACE. . . . KNOCKING HIM SILLY INSTANTLY!

7
A Warning Unheeded

At departure time the following morning the cold snap had eased some. That was not necessarily good news for Boris and his flock. As temperatures rise near and above the freezing mark, snow storms are often on the horizon.

Boris had positioned himself on higher ground again by the lake to address the flock just before take-off. His final instructions included some serious words of caution, most particularly for the younger, first-timer ducks. Lil' Manny and Everett were side by side, standing on the frozen ground just below Boris.

"We should be on the mighty Mississippi River before noon today," Boris said. "Our first stop will be just a few miles upstream from Bettendorf, Iowa. The river's nice and wide there—almost a mile, in fact. We'll land out near the middle where the main current is the swiftest. Surface feeding is usually excellent there, and it's safer! If any duck hunters come out in their scullboats we'll have a good chance of seeing them. It takes a long time for a scullboat to reach us from shore.

"But don't be lulled into any delusions by the word, 'safer,'" Boris warned. "One reason duck hunters use scullboats on the river this time of year is because they know we ducks always land way out on the river to feed. We have no choice, of course, when the river's edge is all ice and the ground covered with frozen snow. But these are hazards we ducks face daily on long trips like this.

"Now you youngsters may ask, 'What's a scullboat?' Good question! Just ask any old timer next to you and he'll tell you a scullboat is trouble—real trouble! It's not a rowboat, nor is it a motorboat. If duck hunters used either of these we'd see or hear them. No sir! A scullboat is like no other boat. It's low, it's flat and silent, and it's sneaky! Why sneaky? Because the bough of the boat is always covered heavily with branches just to make it look like only a pile of floating brush. The duck hunter moves the boat through the water with a single oar sticking out a hole in the stern. He uses a kind of lazy-8 wrist movement so there's almost no splashing with the oar. That's how he can sneak up on us often undetected. So unless you can tell the difference between a real pile of floating brush coming at you and a scullboat covered with brush, you're a dead duck! So listen up now—real good!

"First, a real pile of floating brush floats lower in the water. Second, if a brush pile is floating across the current instead of down current, it's a phony! And lastly, if a brush pile is moving at you faster than the current, you can bet your best hay seeds it's a duck hunter in a scullboat! And the duck hunter usually attacks us from upstream to use the down current to gain speed. So if you see anything like this, get your tail up off the water as fast as you can!

"I might also add here, unfortunately, that if any of you only get wounded in a fracas such as I have just described, you're probably still a goner because in most scullboats there is a dog that can swim like a fish. He'll jump in the cold water and bring you back to his master in his teeth!

"So that's about it," Boris concluded. "And I hope you first-timer ducks were really paying attention. Any questions?"

All of the ducks were silent.

"Okay, then—be careful out there! Oh, wait! There's one more thing. Lil' Manny made a new friend yesterday, a young snow goose who just lost his flock. His name is Everett. Since Everett is now alone, Lil' Manny asked me if Everett could travel with us to the Gulf. Of course I said 'Yes'."

The breaking dawn was streaking across the cold winter sky now, reflecting brightly on Boris's emerald green head. "That's about it!" he said waving a huge wing to all of the ducks—and Everett. "Let's move out!"

In a flash of beating wings and whistling wind, the flock of wild mallards was airborne once again. Along with a lone white snow goose trailing close behind Lil' Manny.

For the first couple of hours Lil' Manny seemed to be keeping up with the flock. Then suddenly, the little duck began to falter in the sky, dipping up and down most seriously. This time it appeared the exhausting flight was finally doing him in.

Everett was the first to notice. "Missy!" he honked loudly as he flew past Mandrake. "He's having great difficulty keeping up with us." Both the snow goose and Missy dropped back next to Lil' Manny.

"I think I see the Mississippi River up ahead," Missy exclaimed. "Do you think you can make it there?" she asked.

"I'm awfully tired but I'll try."

Missy was worried sick now and Everett felt helpless. Something had to be done. "I'm going to fly ahead and tell Martha, Everett," Missy shouted. "Maybe she can get Boris to land the flock on the river right away—stay with him!" Immediately the little hen increased her speed to catch the flock as Lil' Manny and Everett drifted farther and farther behind.

"I may not be able to take off again once we land," Lil' Manny confided in Everett. "I just don't have any lift anymore and I'm beginning to ache all over."

"Hang in there, Mandrake!" Everett said encouragingly. "You and I have to get to the Gulf together!"

Lil' Manny did not answer the snow goose. He needed every ounce of energy just to stay in the sky.

"There—over there!" Everett shouted. "I see the flock now! They're down on the river . . . out near the middle. Let's go join them, my friend."

Lil' Manny dropped almost too fast, belly landing in a spray of icy water some distance from the main flock. Everett splashed in directly behind him.

"Well, we made it down!" the snow goose said proudly. "Now we can rest and feed."

Soon Martha and Missy came swimming up, followed quickly by Boris. "How are you feeling, son?" his mother asked anxiously.

"I saw you both drop back," Boris said. Nothing got past the old mallard. "Are you okay?"

"I'm a little pooped," Lil' Manny said wearily. He was just too tired to pretend any longer.

This time Boris was very concerned about Lil' Manny's weakening condition, but he refused to show any emotion. "I think we'll rest here on the river for a few hours," he said, "before we push on. I'll check in on you again before we take off." With that the big drake jumped into the air and flew low across the water to rejoin his flock. One more time Lil' Manny was saved, at least temporarily.

For the next hour or so the wild mallards chased floating insects on the swift current or just frolicked about having fun dodging half submerged limbs and brush. Eventually, they separated into two main groups, with many of the younger ducks swimming upstream some fifty yards from Boris and most of the older ducks downstream.

QUACKING A PANICKY WARNING AS LOUD AS HE COULD, BORIS SPRANG FROM THE RIVER AND FLEW TOWARD THE YOUNGER DUCKS AT LIGHTNING SPEED—BUT HE WAS TOO LATE!

Seriously concerned about Lil' Manny's welfare, Martha and Missy and Jenny swam with Lil' Manny and Everett. All four mallards and the snow goose were farther downstream, a good distance from both of the other groups of ducks.

None of the flock noticed a rather large cluster of branches come sliding quietly into the group of younger ducks upstream. No one, that is, except Boris!

Quacking a panicky warning, Boris sprang from the river and with lightening speed flew low across the water toward the group of younger ducks—

43

but he was too late! Just as the young ducks began to lift off from the river, a lone duck hunter raised up from behind the deceptive pile of floating brush with a double-barreled shotgun, then fired two exploding shells directly into the flock of ducks.

Orange fire, thick puffs of blue smoke and hot lead split the morning stillness as two ducks dropped mortally wounded into the river. While the duck hunter's dog swam through the chilling waters to retrieve the two dead ducks for his master, another wounded duck limped helplessly toward the shoreline.

High in the sky overhead the remaining flock circled with frustration. A count was soon taken.

Because they were far from the tragic scene, Lil' Manny and his mother and Missy and Everett were safe. Missy's mother, Missus Missy Prissy and the rest of Lil' Manny's family were also safe swimming farther downstream with the older ducks.

Hector managed to survive too, even though he was caught in the heat of battle with the reckless younger ducks. But he was scared out of his wits when the hunter's shotgun shells exploded right next to him and would always remember it. From that day forward, Hector's attitude greatly improved, along with his respect for those with more experience. 'Hector-the-heckler' soon became a nickname he would gladly loose.

But where in the world was Boris?

Now circling high above the river with the rest of the flock, Lil' Manny looked down to see a lone drake flapping desperately to reach shore—it was Boris!

"Momma!" Lil' Manny cried. "That's Boris down there, just over the river heading for shore. He's hurt and he needs my help!"

Martha realized the seriousness of the situation, but she also knew there was nothing anyone could do to save Boris. The duck hunter had already picked up his dog from the cold water and was sculling toward the shoreline as fast as he could, anticipating about where the big mallard would crash-land. "There's nothing we can do, son!" his mother shouted. "Save yourself! Let's just all fly out of here as fast as our wings will carry us!"

"I can't do that, Momma!" Lil' Manny hollered back. "I can't let Boris die like this, somebody has to help him!"

"Don't waste your life, too, Mandrake," she cried, "please don't!" In her heart Martha knew how her son felt about Boris.

Missy, who was circling nearby pleaded with Lil' Manny, "Please don't leave us, Mandrake," she pleaded. "We need you—and I love you!" She began to cry softly.

"I'm sorry, Missy . . . Momma," Lil' Manny said, "but I have to try. I know Boris would have done the same for me. Harold will take over the flock now and get you all to the Gulf. Please follow him and do whatever he asks."

Then the little duck flew closer to the snow goose. Confiding in him privately, he confessed, "Everett, my new wonderful friend, the time has come. If Boris has any chance at all to survive he'll need my help . . . and we both know I could not have gone on much farther anyway. Please watch out for my mother and Missy and Jenny until you all reach the Gulf."

"But—" Everett stammered.

"Take heart!" Lil' Manny said. "This may not be the end. If Boris is not too badly hurt and we can hide and feed somewhere for awhile until he heals and I grow stronger, we may make the Gulf yet!" He waved a wing to all, "Goodbyyyyyyyyye . . ." With total disregard for his own life, Lil' Manny then dived headlong down toward the faltering Boris.

WITH TOTAL DISREGARD FOR HIS OWN LIFE, LIL' MANNY DIVED HEAD-LONG DOWN TOWARD THE FALTERING BORIS!

8
Beavers to the Rescue

"Go back, my boy! Go back!" Boris shouted to Lil' Manny who was now flying just ahead of the wounded mallard. "Save yourself before it's too late!"

"I can't do that, Boris!" Lil' Manny shouted back. "You're hurt and I want to help you!" The two ducks were fast approaching the edge of the river. "Follow me!" Lil' Manny cried. "We'll hide in the brush in the water next to the bank!"

Too weak to argue and only half conscious with blurring vision, Boris followed the young drake's low flying image ahead of him until both ducks crash-landed next to a mound of branches protruding from the water.

Unfortunately, the duck hunter in his scullboat arrived at the same place at the same time. Standing now behind the brush covered bow of his boat he took aim at the two ducks. "GOTCHA, NOW!" he cried. But in the split second it took him to fire both barrels, both ducks suddenly disappeared from the water—as if by magic! And when the blue smoke cleared from the spent shells, the ducks were no where to be seen. Not even a single feather was floating. The only visible signs of any shooting at all were a few ripples from the shot-gun blasts and the quiet gurgle of a few bubbles rising from beneath the river's surface where the two ducks once sat.

Needless to say, the duck hunter was exasperated and began to circle the watery thicket in a desperate attempt to find his prey. When he was unsuccessful after a thorough search, he disgustedly rowed his scullboat back on to the open river.

So where did Lil' Manny and Boris disappear to? The answer to that question was a surprise to both ducks. Neither had suspected the mound of branches they crash-landed next to was actually the home of a family of beavers. And it was the beavers who saved the two ducks' lives.

The rescue plan began when Baxter Beaver, the poppa beaver of the family, had been paddling with his big tail around his home when he saw the two mallards and the scullboat approach. The ducks erratic flying told him immediately they were in real trouble. Diving into his water tunnel to his home he quickly related to his wife, Bernice, what was about to take place. At once, both beavers swam out from their home, then hid in the water just below the surface, anticipating about where they expected the ducks would splash down. An instant before the duck hunter fired his shotgun, the beavers jerked both ducks under water, then guided them into their home of branches through their private water tunnel beneath the surface.

And that is how the two mallards were rescued from their impending fate—at the last split second by two wonderful beavers.

Once inside the beaver home, Lil' Manny and Boris were introduced to the beaver family, Baxter and his wife, Bernice, and their two children, Becky and Benny Beaver.

"I don't know how we can ever thank you for saving our lives," Lil' Manny said gratefully. "My friend here, Boris, was the lead duck of our flock and he's just been shot by a duck hunter. We were gonners for sure if you hadn't pulled us under the water!"

"Well we're glad we could help," Baxter Beaver said. "Duck hunters have taken a shot or two at us in the past, too, but fortunately we're still here." The beaver slowly stroked his hairy chin with his paw, careful to avoid his two very sharp and protruding front teeth. "But now we have to figure out what to do next," he said. "You guys need some place safe to recuperate for awhile."

"How badly are you hurt, Boris?" Bernice Beaver asked.

"It's my left wing," Boris said. "It feels like it may be broken—but I hope not."

"Let's take a look," Lil' Manny said as he gently examined the wing. "It looks like maybe just a bad splinter." He removed some lead pellets with his bill,

IN THEIR WATER THICKET HOME, THE BEAVER FAMILY LISTEN INTENTLY
TO MANDRAKE AND BORIS'S HARROWING TALE

then spit them out. "There! Now at least there shouldn't be any lead poison-
ing, but of course I can't be sure. Remember, I'm a duck—not a doctor!"

Everyone laughed.

In spite of Boris's aching wing, he enjoyed Lil' Manny's humor. "This little duck always seems to see the brighter side of life," he said to the Beavers.
"And he has tremendous courage. He left our flock just to save me!"

Baxter Beaver looked at Lil' Manny. "That was a fine and noble thing you
did, lad," he said, "and you should be commended. But what happened to all
of your feathers?"

"He's just had a little trouble fully developing by flight time," Boris said. "But I'm sure he'll grow big and strong if we can just find a place to hide out for the time being."

"I have an idea," Baxter said, "but it's a long shot!"

"Anything!" Lil' Manny said. "We'll try anything!"

"Well, did you guys happen to see that farm about a mile from here before you had your accident on the river?" the beaver asked.

"Yes we did," Boris said, "and I think I know what you're thinking. Somehow we have to get to that farm, that is if they have domestic mallards there."

"You got it!" Baxter said, "and yes, they do have a whole flock of tame mallards on that farm. I've seen them!"

Lil' Manny looked puzzled. "What good will that do?" he asked.

"Wild mallards can sometimes mix in with tame mallards," Boris said, "if the tame mallards agree. Then if we don't get caught by the farmer or his family while you grow and I heal, we could possibly make it to the Gulf, eventually. . . . if I can make it to the farm *first*, that is," he questioned soberly.

"Has that ever been tried before, Boris?" Lil' Manny asked.

"Very successfully," Boris answered, "by your very own grandfather, Mandrake I, before he became a famous lead duck. By the way," he said turning to the Beavers, "this little drake is Mandrake II, the grandson of Mandrake I. Have you ever heard of him?"

"Yes we surely have!" Mr. and Mrs. Beaver answered in unison.

"And we know about his super track record as a lead duck," Baxter said. "It is indeed a pleasure to meet the grandson of such a famous mallard duck."

Lil' Manny was embarrassed. He wanted to get back to Boris's story. "So tell me more about how my grandfather came to live with some tame mallards, Boris," he asked. Everyone listened as Boris related the story.

"It was so simple it was funny," Boris began. "And it's the story of how Mandrake I met and fell in love with a domestic mallard hen, your grandmother, Greta," he said, turning to Lil' Manny.

"Really?" Lil' Manny said surprised.

"It's true!" Boris said. "Some years ago, before Mandrake I was elected lead duck, his flock was en route to the Gulf just like we are today. They all landed in a corn field to feed, somewhere along this river, I think. A group of tame mallards from a nearby farm came out to investigate, and in the group was a beautiful young mallard hen named Greta. And whamo! Instant love for Mandrake I and Greta! But Greta's wing had been clipped, like all domestic ducks wings are clipped periodically to keep them from flying away. So your grandfather, clever duck that he was, decided to mix in with the tame mallards and pretend that he was one of them until Greta's feathers had grown back enough for her to fly. Then just before the farmer came out one morning to clip all of his ducks wings again, Mandrake I and your grandmother, Greta, zoomed off into the sky."

"wow! That's some story, Boris," Lil' Manny said. "I'm glad you told me."

"I was just waiting for the right time," Boris said, "and this looks like it!"

Lil' Manny's courage surfaced again. "If my grandfather did it, so can we, Boris!"

"Well, son," Boris said rather sadly. "While I appreciate your optimism and courage, I'm in pretty bad shape to hike a mile through snow and ice. And neither of us can fly very well, remember?"

"But we have to try, Boris!" Lil' Manny said. "It's our only chance."

"The lad's right," Baxter Beaver said.

Boris admired Lil' Manny' pluckiness. "Well, I guess it is our only chance, but we'll have to wait until dark. If we're spotted in the daylight by a dog or some other predator, we'll be two dead ducks!"

"It's settled then," Baxter Beaver said. "You guys rest up here until dark while me and my family go for a swim. When you're ready to go, I'll give you some directions, but it will be tough going at night, I can tell you that for sure."

"I think they can make it with this little duck leading the way," Bernice Beaver said. "After all, he *is* the grandson of a very famous mallard duck."

Boris reviewed the slim chance in his mind. Two very weak and tired ducks, tramping a mile through ice and snow at night, climbing up over and under logs and razor sharp fences, crossing frozen streams and ravines—not very good odds, really! But then, what else could they do? "I guess we'll go for it," he finally said. "And we appreciate resting up here until dark. You folks have been very kind to us. You are a wonderful family of beavers."

"It has been our pleasure to meet such brave ducks," Bernice Beaver said.

"Yes you are!" the two little Beavers chimed in.

"Then we'll go have that swim now," Baxter Beaver said, "and we'll see you guys in a little while. With that, the Beaver family disappeared down their water tunnel.

Farther south, with Harold now temporarily leading Boris's flock, the rest of the ducks were beating their way to the Gulf with heavy heart. With two ducks already lost, most of the remaining ducks were convinced they had seen Boris and Lil' Manny for the last time.

Understandably, Martha, Missy, Jenny and Everett were heartbroken at Lil' Manny's sacrifice for Boris. Yet all knew in their hearts why the little drake had been so heroic and self-sacrificing—even though they were almost certain his attempt would be futile and the lives of the two wonderful mallards probably sealed forever.

Missy fought beck tears of pain and heartache. "Oh, Martha," she cried as she continued to beat her wings through the cold wind, "how could this terrible thing happen to Mandrake? He was so sweet and kind. I know I truly love him now, but it's too late! He's gone from my life . . . forever," she moaned.

"You must be brave now, Missy," Martha said trying to console the young hen. "Mandrake would have wanted that. He was very fond of you, you know. He told me once that if anything happened to him we must all go on living our lives."

"He told me that, too!" Everett said proudly flying close to the mallard hens. "And who knows, folks? Mandrake may still be alive somewhere. He's one smart duck and he may just fool all the other ducks yet" Even though the snow goose may have questioned what he had just said, he knew the mallard hens needed some hope and faith right now, more than ever.

Jenny was sick at heart over the loss of her youngest brother whom she had just begun to understand and love. Could Everett maybe be right? she asked herself. Could my little brother still be alive—somewhere? She prayed it was true.

The three mallard hens and the snow goose flew on in silence now. Only the whistling wind around their beating wings broke that silence.

When the Beaver family returned to their home, darkness was falling. Unfortunately, so was a new snow storm.

"I'm afraid I have some rather dreary news," Baxter Beaver said waking Lil' Manny and Boris. "There's a new snow storm brewing outside and that could make your hike even tougher."

"Perhaps you should stay the night with us," Bernice Beaver said.

"Oh, goodie! Can they Momma?" the Beaver children asked excitedly.

"I appreciate your offer, mam," Boris said testing his left wing for any strength, "but Mandrake and I must leave tonight. As you know, a brewing snow storm can last for days—even weeks this time of year."

It was the first time Boris had called Lil' Manny, Mandrake. In spite of his still scrawny size, Mandrake was beginning to feel like a full-fledged mallard drake. "Boris is right," he said. "It's now or never." He turned to Boris. "Ready when you are, sir!"

After Baxter Beaver reminded the ducks to always head northwest to find the farm, Mandrake and Boris expressed their indebtedness one more time. Then they dove down the Beaver's water tunnel and surfaced to the outside world, a world of darkness, freezing wind and slashing snow.

"How's your wing, Boris?" Mandrake asked as the ducks began to swim to shore.

Boris tried to lift his left wing. Nothing moved. "I was afraid of that," he said remorsefully. "It's numb! Now we'll have to hike the whole way to the farm and I'll have a devil of a time keeping up with you. Maybe you should—"

"If you're thinking of giving up, Boris, forget it!" Mandrake said sternly. "We're going to make it together—all the way!"

Because Mandrake was so insistent, Boris knew he must at least try. After all, wasn't it he who had preached all summer to the little duck that self-confidence, coupled with faith and belief can often overcome great obstacles? A lesson Mandrake had obviously learned very well.

Making the short swim to shore was easy for both ducks. Nobody swims like a duck. But, take a duck out of water—and ask him to climb a slippery riverbank in a snow storm at night—well, that's another problem entirely!

But Mandrake was determined to get the old mallard on shore. With his very large webbed feet braced against some snow covered rocks and his back positioned against Boris's rear end, the little duck pushed with all his might. Sliding, slipping and spinning in the wet snow, the two ducks finally crawled up onto the river bank, then waddled off into the cold and snowy night with Boris dragging his injured wing.

Only once in awhile could the ducks cover any short distances flying, until Boris complained about his wing and would crash-land in the deep snow. Most of the time all they could do was hike, with an occasional hop or two.

Their struggle to reach the farm continued hour after hour after hour, hopefully in the right direction. Mandrake's natural duck instincts were really being tested now. Boris was of little help. Dragging his injured wing in pain brought him almost to the point of delirium, at which time he would insist the two ducks were going in the wrong direction, then wander off aimlessly. Then Mandrake would catch up with him and point him in the right direction.

Finally, after climbing in and out of countless frozen ravines, crawling under dozens of barbed wire fences and stumbling across endless stubbled corn fields, Boris had had enough. Just below one more long hill that lay ahead, he fell defeated in the deep snow—ready to end it all.

"I can't go any farther, Mandrake!" he cried. "My wing's totally numb and I'm frozen from head to foot! Go on—save yourself!"

"Wait here a minute, Boris," the little duck said. "I can still fly a little so I'm going to the top of this hill and take a look." Hopping into the air, he flew the short distance, then looked through the blowing snow across what appeared to be a valley. Not too encouraging so far, he told himself. But then, when he looked down the hill, his heart leaped with joy. Almost directly below him through slanting, blowing snow he could make out the farm the two ducks

WITH HIS LARGE WEBBED FEET BRACED AGAINST SOME ROCKS AND
HIS BACK POSITIONED AGAINST BORIS'S REAR END, THE LITTLE DUCK
PUSHED WITH ALL HIS MIGHT!

had been searching for all night! He shouted back to the wounded mallard
behind him.

"WE MADE IT, BORIS—WE MADE IT! JUST BELOW THIS HILL THERE'S A FARM,
BUILDINGS, TWINKLING LIGHTS—EVERYTHING!"

55

Boris could hardly believe his ears. "ARE YOU SURE?" he shouted as best he could.

"YES, YES, YES!" Mandrake answered. "COME ON UP, BORIS! YOU CAN MAKE IT NOW!"

From somewhere, Boris found one more ounce of strength, then dragged his aching cold body up the short hill to Mandrake. Looking down through the falling snow he saw the farm at last—all covered in white. And it was real!

"Thank goodness," he said weakly. "I thought I was a gonner for sure this time!"

9
Nathan and Delbert

As the two mallards stood on the hill looking down at the farm below, the snow suddenly stopped. Then a pink and orange sky began to form in the east, painted by the morning sun rising behind the hills. Now all of the farm buildings were clearly visible through the crisp morning air.

Boris spoke first. "That barn down there on the left will house the farmer's horses and cows, and that slanted shed next to the barn will be where they keep their domestic fowl, all of the chickens and geese—and the tame mallards. That's the building we have to get into if we have any chance at all," he added, "and I hope the mallards are friendly."

"Let's go!" Mandrake cried.

Boris hesitated. "Not so fast, my boy!" he said. "I think the time has come for you to officially take charge. I can hardly move my wing let alone the rest of me . . . and it's impossible for me to fly. So you fly down and check things out. I'll wait here on the hill." The old drake looked Mandrake straight in the eye. "From now on, you're the lead duck! I nominate you and vote you in unanimously. You've already proven to me you are a true leader—just like your grandfather was."

Suddenly, the moment Mandrake had only dreamed of was a reality. To be appointed lead duck at his young age by such a courageous and experienced duck as Boris, well that was really something—whether by just one vote or not! "Thank you for your confidence in me, Boris," Mandrake said proudly. "I promise to do my best!"

"I know you will, my boy . . . just be careful down there. With the lights on in that shed the farmer or one of his family is probably already collecting eggs. It's about that time—early dawn. Watch out for dogs, too! There are almost always one or two around a farm." As weak and as cold as Boris was he was still teaching, and he could not help but feel very proud of his former student.

"I'll be careful!" Mandrake said. Then he jumped into the air and glided silently down the hill, easily clearing a fence buried in snow next to the hillside.

Boris remained partially hidden in the deep snow with only his bright emerald head sticking up just enough to keep an eye on Mandrake. Then he waited. "Hope he makes it inside," Boris mumbled to himself. "If I have to stay up here in this wet snow much longer, I'll freeze to death for sure!"

Landing in the deep snow next to the shed, Mandrake heard human voices coming from within. Hopping up onto some snow covered creates stacked below a window, he peered inside. As predicted by Boris, a man and a woman

HOPPING UP ONTO SOME SNOW COVERED CRATES STACKED BELOW A WINDOW, MANDRAKE PEERED INSIDE

were collecting eggs from under chickens nesting in straw boxes along one wall. In a dark corner of an opposite wall, dozens of tame mallards and a few geese were quacking quietly.

"Good!" Mandrake whispered to himself. "Lots of mallards." Then he continued to search the rest of the shed, looking for any problems. Suddenly, there it was! In another corner of the shed snoozing in the straw a dog so big Mandrake at first thought it was a small bear. "That could be real trouble!" he told himself.

Just then the man and woman headed for the shed door, their steel buckets filled with golden brown eggs. "Okay, sleepy head," the woman called to the big dog. "Let's go! We got more chores to do."

The big dog stirred and squeaked his eyes open from under layers and layers of thick skin. Then he closed them again. It was just too early.

"C'mon you lazy bloodhound!" the woman repeated more sternly. "No breakfast for anyone 'til we milk the cows—an' that means none for you either, Marvin!"

The word breakfast triggered Marvin's long, limp ears. Slowly he raised himself on all four, blinked his eyes, yawned a long yawn and shook his massive body wildly. Loose skin rolled across his big frame like waves on a stormy sea.

Mandrake ducked his head down below the window ledge. He was taking no chances on being seen by anything so big and ferocious looking. Soon the man and woman and their dog left the shed and were about to pass directly by Mandrake. He quickly dropped down behind the crates in the nick of time. When the couple and their dog disappeared through an open gate, Mandrake saw his chance and flew to the shed door. Because the door was hanging loosely from rusty hinges, the little drake easily squeezed inside.

The chickens saw Mandrake first but only responded with low, nervous cackling. Chickens are like that, cackling low and nervously about everything— and nothing. But when two large tame mallard drakes saw Mandrake, they spoke up loud and clear.

"Who are you?" one said. "You're not part of our flock!"

"And what are you doing in our shed?" the other drake demanded.

Now Mandrake had to do some tall, fast talking. "I'm a wild mallard," he said quickly. "My name is Mandrake, but please, before you start quacking an alarm, hear me out! We need your help, me and my friend, Boris, another wild mallard up on the hill behind us. He's hurt! He was shot by a duck hunter yesterday morning on the river, then the beavers, Baxter and Bernice saved us . . . then last night we hiked here on foot because Boris can't fly an'—"

"Hold it! Hold it! A little slower please!" the first drake interrupted. "Now tell us, where are you guys from?"

"And where are you headed?" the second drake asked.

"We're from up in Canada where we spent the spring and summer," Mandrake said. "I was hatched there in April. We were heading south with our flock for the winter when our lead duck, Boris, who's up on the hill freezing to death got shot trying to warn some first-timer ducks they, too, were about to get shot when—"

"You don't look so good yourself," the second mallard said. "Have you been sick?"

"Goodness, no!" Mandrake said. "I just got a late start and I wasn't in my shell as long as most ducklings. I can't fly very far either, but I'll be okay when I can grow a little mor—"

"You guys hiked here on foot?" the first mallard asked somewhat astonished. "All the way from the river and in the snow storm last night?"

"And with one guy wounded, too!" the other mallard said. "Boy! You guys are really gutsy!"

"Yes, we did!" Mandrake repeated. "But right now, I've got to get Boris off that freezing hill if you'll please help us."

The first mallard was moved by Mandrake's story. "My name is Nathan," he said then nodded to the other mallard, "and this is my brother, Delbert."

"It's nice to meet both of you," Mandrake said. "Now please, can you help us?" It was obvious to Mandrake that Nathan and his brother were speaking for all of the other mallards who stood quietly by listening.

"If the Beavers took you guys in you must be okay," Nathan said. "Baxter and Bernice Beaver are pretty particular whom they share their home with." He turned to his brother, "What do you think, Delbert?"

"Okay with me," Delbert said shrugging his feathered shoulders.

"Good!" Nathan said. "Then go get your buddy before he freezes up there, Mandrake, and we'll see if we can thaw him out. Then we'll take a look at his gun shot wound."

"Thank you! Thank you very much!" Mandrake said as he squeezed himself out the door. "We'll be back soon." In a flash he was winging his way up the snowy hill.

"That's some duck," Nathan said, "for a scrawny little guy. He must love his lead duck very much."

"We mallards have to stick together, tame or wild," Delbert added. "Just like always."

"I've got great news, Boris!" Mandrake shouted as he landed next to the old mallard who now lay almost buried in snow.

"What—what is it?" Boris asked weakly.

"The mallards in the shed down there, they said they'd help us! Isn't that great!"

"I'm in pretty bad shape now, my boy," Boris replied. "I don't even know if I can make it down this hill."

"You don't have to hike down," Mandrake said. "All you have to do is slide!" Without warning, the little drake snapped his bill to Boris's good wing, then tugged with all his might. The old mallard was too weak to resist. After a few hard pulls, Mandrake had Boris at the edge of the hill just above the farm. Then he gave the old mallard a really big shove! Sliding like a bob sled out of control, Boris rocketed down the steep slope in a shower of snow with the little duck flying low overhead. Because of his uncontrollable speed, Boris barely clipped the top of the snow-buried fence at the bottom of the hill, then tumbled upside down into a snow bank next to the shed. Only his long yellow bill and two big orange feet were still sticking out of the snow.

When Mandrake dug the old mallard out he could hardly keep from laughing. Then once again the little duck tugged and pushed with all his might, this time with Boris's help, until the two ducks finally reached the shed door.

Forcing Boris's big green head through the wide crack at the bottom of the door, Mandrake again braced himself against the old mallard's rear end. With

ALTHOUGH BORIS PICKED UP A LOT OF SPEED FROM THE STEEP HILL, HE WAS SAVED AT THE BOTTOM BY A DEEP PILE OF SNOW AGAINST THE SHED. HE TUMBLED INTO IT UPSIDE DOWN.

a tremendous push, the door shifted on its rusty hinges, allowing Boris to wedge himself inside. Mandrake tumbled in behind.

"This must be Boris!" Nathan said smiling. "Welcome to our humble abode, wild mallards. Of course we've already met Mandrake," Nathan continued, turning to Boris, "so let me introduce us. I'm Nathan and this is my brother, Delbert."

"Our house is your house," Delbert grinned.

"Thank—thank you," Boris said weakly. He was almost too cold to speak.

Mandrake beamed. At last he and Boris had been rescued from the freezing cold.

"We already know your story, Boris," Nathan continued, "thanks to your dear and loyal friend here, Mandrake." He paused briefly with a slight frown. "But we have an immediate problem to confront before we invite you to dine and drink, after which time I'll look at your wound, Boris. The farmer's wife is due back here any minute to feed and water all of us, so I suggest you hide in the straw over there," he pointed to a dark corner with his large wing, "until she leaves. My brother will help cover you up."

"What about that big dog I saw through the window?" Mandrake asked.

"Ah, you're referring to Marvin, the bloodhound of course," Nathan said. "He seldom accompanies the wife. Marvin and the farmer are closer. They used to be hunting buddies together when Marvin was younger and had all his faculties."

"My brother means when Marvin's sniffer was really good," Delbert said, "but he can't smell too good anymore and his eye sight is not the best. But he tries, and he can put on quite a show for the farmer. He's fun to watch!"

"Actually, Marvin has become quite friendly in his old age," Nathan said, "now that he can't hunt seriously anymore. In fact, he likes everybody, you'll see."

"Well, that's a relief!". Mandrake sighed. "Boris and I sure don't need a big bloodhound chasing us all over the place. I thought at first he was a bear!"

Everyone laughed.

"I'm certain you have nothing to fear from Marvin," Nathan said. "I've seen him with strangers. All he does is sniff them a bit. But let's get back to hiding you guys. Delbert, cover these ducks in the straw right now—before we're all in trouble!"

"Come, Mandrake!" Boris said finally beginning to thaw out. "Let's do as they ask." The old drake waddled to a dark corner of the shed dragging his injured wing. Mandrake was close behind.

No sooner had Delbert covered the two wild mallards with straw when the shed door opened. It was the farmer's wife with a bucket of grain, and as Nathan had predicted, no Marvin.

ACTUALLY, MARVIN HAS BECOME QUITE FRIENDLY IN HIS OLD AGE . . . IN FACT, HE LIKES EVERYBODY, YOU'LL SEE!

"Here chicky, chick, chicks," she called. "Here ducky, duck, ducks . . . come and get it!"

Everyone gathered around quacking and clucking softly as they gobbled up the grain. When the bucket was empty, the farmer's wife left as quickly as she had come, this time leaving the shed door open.

"So far so good!" Mandrake said to Boris.

10

Guess Who's Related

"**O**kay, you guys can come out now!" Nathan cried. "The coast is clear! Come join us for food and drink."

Mandrake and Boris crawled out from under the straw, then eagerly joined the ducks and geese and chickens who were now eating furiously.

"Help yourself!" Delbert said to the wild mallards. "You guys must be starved!"

When everyone was full and resting, Nathan said to Boris, "Let me take a look at that injured wing of yours." Boris stood quietly as Nathan did his examination.

"How does it look to you, Nathan?" Mandrake asked.

"It appears you were right, Mandrake. There's only a splintered bone, nothing broken and probably not too serious. He should be up and around in a couple of days, but he won't do any flying for weeks."

"That's too long!" Boris said discouragingly. "How can we possibly hide here for weeks?"

"Just leave that to us," Delbert said positively. "We know the routine of the farmer and his wife like the back of our webbed foot! Every morning is the same, just like this morning . . . until they decide to clean out the shed again which shouldn't be for several weeks or a month. They just did it yesterday.

"Of course they do take a chicken for Sunday dinner almost every weekend, but seldom a duck or goose. We're reserved for special occasions like Christmas or Easter when they have family over."

"Doesn't that make you nervous when the holidays get near?" Mandrake asked.

"Sure! For the other ducks and geese," Nathan answered. "And a lot of them are also sold to other farmers, along with eggs from the hens. But me and Delbert are too old and too tough to eat now. So they just keep us around to make more ducks. That's about it.

"Now while the rest of us go outside for some fresh morning air, why don't you two guys get some rest? We'll be right outside to warn you if necessary, okay?"

"We do need some rest," Boris said, "and I've got some thawing out to do. Thanks for everything. You're swell ducks."

"Thanks from me, too," Mandrake added.

"You're both welcome, "Nathan said as all of the other ducks and geese— and a few chickens—piled out the door.

Later that night Nathan and Delbert and Mandrake and Boris met near the shed door to discuss the two wild mallards future while everyone else was asleep. During their whispered conversation, Boris told Nathan and Delbert how Mandrake had unselfishly risked his life to save him.

Mandrake was embarrassed and modified Boris's story, explaining to the two tame mallards that he could not have flown much farther anyway, considering his weakened physical condition; that he simply accompanied Boris across the river until the two ducks could find a hiding place away from the approaching duck hunter.

Boris ignored Mandrake's modesty, then asked the two duck brothers if they had ever heard of the famous lead mallard drake, Mandrake I.

"Heard of him?" Nathan said. "We *knew* him! He was right here on *this* very Iowa farm!"

"You're kidding!" Boris said.

"Nope!" Nathan said. "He was *here!*"

"My grandfather was here on this farm?" Mandrake asked astonished.

"Mandrake I was *your* grandfather?" Delbert asked wide-eyed.

"That's right!" Boris said pointing to Mandrake. "This young drake is Mandrake II, the grandson of Mandrake I!"

"Golly!" Delbert said. "What a surprise!"

"And what a coincidence!" Nathan said.

"And there's more!" Delbert said, almost too loudly.

"I don't know how you can top this story," Boris replied.

"Well . . . how about this!" Nathan smiled. "We're related to Mandrake here!"

"You've got to be joking!" Mandrake said in total disbelief.

"'No' again," Nathan said. "Your grandmother, Greta, was our aunt, mine and Delbert's, Mandrake, so that makes us Greta's nephews, and guess what? Second cousins to you! How about that!"

"Wow! What a wonderful surprise!" Mandrake said. "Finding my real cousins here on a farm in Iowa! I'm really happy to meet you, *cousins!*" He turned to Boris. "Nobody will ever believe this," he said grinning. "Boy! It certainly is a small world, isn't it?"

"And it's getting smaller!" Nathan laughed. "Now tomorrow's another day, boys, so I think we'd all better get some shut-eye if we're going to out-fox the farmer and his wife with this plan of ours."

"There you go again, Nathan," Delbert said shaking his head nervously. "I hate foxes! Just the word scares the living daylights out of me!"

"I'm sorry, Delbert," Nathan said. "I forgot."

"Are there a lot of foxes around here?" Mandrake asked.

"A few," Nathan answered casually, "but they terrorize my brother when one gets in here."

"How do they get in?" Boris asked.

"The same way you did," Nathan said, "through that loose door."

"Isn't the farmer aware of this?"

"He knows about it," Delbert said, "and he's always telling his wife he's going to fix it, but he never does. And he just lost another chicken to a fox only two weeks ago! Ugh: It gives me shivers just to think about it!"

"Doesn't all that ruckus bring the farmer?"

"Oh, sure!" Nathan said. "But by the time he hears all the quacking and clucking out here, gets his gun and runs in here, the fox is out the door."

"It's always the same ole fox, too," Delbert added, "and he's real mean and fearless because he knows we're all too frightened to band together and fight

"HEARD OF HIM?" NATHAN CRIED—ALMOST TOO LOUDLY "WE KNEW HIM—WE MET HIM! HE WAS RIGHT HERE ON THIS VERY IOWA FARM!"

back." The tame mallard screwed up his face and shook his head sadly. "So he just takes what he wants—which is usually a nice young chicken."

"My brother tells it about right," Nathan said. "It's too bad we can't band together and scare this foxy devil out of here for good, but nobody wants to start a ruckus with a fox if they aren't backed up by everybody else. It would be suicide!"

"Let's quit talking about it!" Delbert said wiggling his shoulders with fear. "You guys are not helping me sleep tonight."

"See you boys in the morning," Boris said. Then everybody hit the straw.

Close Calls on the Farm

The following morning, as predicted by Delbert, the farmer and his wife returned to collect their eggs. The bloodhound was close behind but today, was anything but sleepy. Instead he was wide awake, even a little frisky for an old dog, putting his nose into almost every chicken nest after the farmer and his wife had collected each egg-much to the aggravation of the chickens who often clucked their disapproval of the dog's cold nose.

Mandrake and Boris were tucked away in the straw in a dark corner again, shaking nervously since it was their first encounter with the farmer and his wife—and the big dog.

While the farmer and his wife were busying themselves with the task at hand, Marvin suddenly decided to take a trip around the shed, including running into the dark corners!

As the big dog approached Mandrake and Boris froze, certain they were about to be discovered. At one point, Marvin was so close his huge paws came within inches of stepping directly on the two ducks! Then to add to the feather-raising experience, the bloodhound stopped dead in his tracks. Lifting his big wrinkled face high in the air, he did some serious sniffing, suggesting he just might be on the trail of something?

The wild ducks began to sweat.

Then at the last second, a rescue call from the farmer's wife: "C'mon, Marvin," she said. "We're done here. Let's go!" Her husband headed out the door.

The big bloodhound hesitated. Sniffing the air again, he tossed his wrinkled head from side to side as his long ears slapped at his face—but he did not look down. Thank goodness!

"What do you think you smell, poor dogey?" the farmer's wife said. "Have you forgotten your nose is not as good as it used to be? C'mon, let's go!"

The bloodhound continued to stall, making another sniffing trip around the shed.

"Okay, that's it, Marvin, I've got chores to do! When you're through check-

MARVIN WAS SO CLOSE, HIS HUGE PAWS CAME WITHIN INCHES
OF STEPPING ON THE TWO DRAKES

ing things out I'll be in the barn." Then she disappeared out the door, leaving it partly open for the big dog to follow.

But Marvin did not follow at once. Instead, he passed by the two hiding mallards one more time, then stopped directly in front of Nathan and Delbert. "What's going on here?" he asked in his deep bass voice.

"YOU KNOW??" Delbert asked.

"Of course!" Marvin answered. "I may not see and sniff as good as I used to but I'm still a bloodhound, remember?"

"Okay! You guys can come out now!" Nathan shouted. "Marvin knows you're here."

Uncertain what the big dog would do next but with no other choice, Mandrake and Boris crawled out of their hiding place and confronted the bloodhound head on. Before either of them could speak, Nathan interceded.

"These are two wild mallards, Mandrake and Boris," he said to Marvin. "We've been hiding them from the farmer and his wife because they had some serious problems on the river yesterday." Then he proceeded to tell Marvin the rest of the two ducks' ordeal while the big dog listened patiently. When Nathan finished, Marvin was sympathetic, much to the surprise and delight of Mandrake and Boris.

"I guess you fellows are lucky to be here at all," the bloodhound said.

"I guess we are, sir," Mandrake said. "Now will you please help us until we can both fly out of here? It shouldn't be more than a few weeks."

"I don't know if that's true," Boris said doubtfully, trying to move his wing.

"Since you're both already friends of Nathan and Delbert, I'll do what I can," Marvin said, "but I can't promise you won't be discovered."

"You did a good job faking it so far, Marvin," Delbert joked. "You sure fooled me when you were running around sniffing the air. You almost stepped on Mandrake and Boris." Everyone laughed.

"Well, now of course you know I saw them hiding in the straw and the farmer and his wife did not," the bloodhound said, "but let's get down to business. I have to join the missus soon or she'll come looking for me."

"You have a plan, Marvin?" Nathan asked.

"I have a suggestion, my dear Nathan," Marvin said.

"What is it?" Delbert asked.

"It seems to me hiding these two wild mallards in the straw every time the farmer and his wife come into the chicken shed is very risky," Marvin said, "very risky indeed. I spotted them in seconds! So I'm still pretty good at my job, no matter what some say." The big bloodhound grinned but with such a wrinkled face, nobody knows for sure when a bloodhound is grinning.

"Sooner or later," Marvin continued, "and probably sooner, they'll be seen hiding and caught. We all know what happens next."

"Sold for a wild duck dinner to someone, right?" Delbert quipped.

"Exactly!" Marvin replied.

"So what is your suggestion?" Nathan repeated.

"Simply mix these two wild ducks with all of you tame mallards now! With some two dozen other mallards in our flock here, including little ones and big ones—and some not looking any more fit than these two do now, they've got a chance to survive." The bloodhound looked at Mandrake and Boris, then back to the two brothers. "It's been done before as you guys know—right here on this very farm and hopefully the farmer's forgotten just what happened."

Nathan and Delbert nodded their heads. "You're speaking of that super lead duck, Mandrake I, right?" Delbert asked.

"Sure!" Marvin answered.

"Well I've got a surprise for you, Marvin," Nathan said pointing to Mandrake. "Meet the grandson of that super lead duck, Mandrake II!"

"I'll be doggone!" Marvin said. "No wonder these guys made it all the way from the river at night in a snow storm—and on foot! That kind of act could only have been done by another Mandrake leading the way!"

"And there's more!" Delbert said excitedly. "You remember Mandrake I flew off with Greta, our mother's sister? So that means Nathan and me are cousins to Mandrake II!"

"That's really *re-barkable*," the big dog said shaking his wrinkled head almost in disbelief. "But now you've got to keep these two guys out of harm's way until they can make it out of here on their own. And I've got to get out of here before they miss me. See you all later." With that, the big bloodhound left the shed.

"He's one fine dog," Mandrake said.

"Yes, and he has a big heart," Nathan said.

"I agree," Boris added.

"And he's going to help Mandrake and Boris!" Delbert cried.

"Don't get too excited yet, Delbert," Nathan said. "They still have a long and treacherous way to go."

For the next few weeks Mandrake and Boris managed to successfully hide themselves among the flock of tame mallards whenever the farmer or his wife came into the shed. When Marvin was along—which was almost every time— the big dog purposely ignored Mandrake and Boris as he roamed among the domestic fowl. Both wild mallards were now looking stronger and healthier every day. Boris's wing was healing and Mandrake's bare skin spots were filling in rapidly with beautiful feathers. His scrawny size was all but gone.

Then early one morning, another test came for the two wild mallards. It all began with a clanging, rattling sound of steel against steel outside the shed door.

"WHAT'S THAT NOISE?" Mandrake asked waking startled.

"It's the farmer and his wife," Nathan replied. "They've come to clean out our shed and bring in fresh straw. The noise you hear is the pitchforks in the wheelbarrow. Now we'll all be chased outside into the pen."

"This could be serious," Boris said, "particularly if Mandrake and I get separated from the rest of you fellows."

"Don't panic!" Nathan soothed. "Just continue as you have before, stay close to the flock so you don't stand out too much."

A lot of quacking and clucking occurred when the farmer entered with his wheelbarrow, followed quickly by his wife and Marvin. With raised arms and shooing cries the farmer and his wife circled the ducks and chickens and chased them into the yard, with Marvin's help, of course. Once again, Mandrake and Boris moved safely among the flock of tame mallards, still unidentified as intruders by the farmer or his wife.

For the next few hours the farmer made trip after trip carrying loads of dirty straw out the door in his wheelbarrow while his wife raked piles of straw inside. When the floor was clean, the farmer returned with loads of fresh straw which his wife then scattered about with her pitchfork.

But just as the farmer was about to push his last load of fresh straw into the shed, he suddenly stopped at the door. Quizzically he observed his flock of mallards all standing about in a corner of the pen. Then he hollered back to his wife inside.

"MARJORIE, HOW MANY MALLARDS DO WE HAVE NOW?"

"I DON'T RIGHTLY KNOW, SAM—WHY?" his wife shouted back.

"DON'T YOU KEEP TRACK OF 'EM?" the farmer asked a bit perturbed.

"WELL, WHEN I CAN," was the reply. "PROBABLY, MAYBE TWENTY-FIVE OR SO—OR MORE?"

The farmer looked hard at Mandrake and Boris for the first time, obviously perplexed. "WELL, THERE'S TWO BIG GREEN-HEADED DRAKES OUT HERE THAT ARE REAL BEAUTS! I WAS JUST THINKIN' ABOUT CHRISTMAS, THAT'S ALL."

The farmer's wife was getting impatient with her husband. "SAM!" she cried, "PLEASE BRING IN THAT LAST LOAD OF STRAW SO WE CAN HAVE SOME LUNCH!"

Ten minutes later the farmer and his wife left the shed, leaving the door ajar for Marvin to follow, eventually. He often stayed behind to check things out thoroughly.

"I suppose you boys know the farmer is finally getting suspicious," Marvin said, "and I'm sure neither Mandrake nor Boris wants to end up on somebody's Christmas platter."

"Then we must leave *before* Christmas!" Mandrake said.

"I'm sure you both will be ready by then," Nathan returned positively.

Boris looked concerned. "I don't know," he said testing his injured wing. "Even if I can fly out of here, making it all the way to the Gulf with Mandrake is doubtful."

"You still have more time to heal, Boris," Delbert said. "It's not Christmas yet!"

"Well, if I'm not ready to go by then," Boris said turning to Mandrake, "you must fly on alone, son. Your family will need you."

"NO WAY!" snapped Mandrake. "We're *both* going . . . all the way!"

"I like Mandrake's spunk!" Delbert said. "He's just like his grandfather."

"Well . . . I guess I better get on back, Marvin said. "I just wanted you all to be aware of the situation. I do believe we have some time yet, but I can't be sure how long. I'll see you all later." Then the big dog trotted out the door.

As the days and weeks added up both wild mallard ducks began to improve, but Mandrake was developing much faster than Boris's wing was healing. Most of his primary feathers had now grown in, he was no longer scrawny looking and his size was almost equal to that of Boris. And the way he jumped into the air occasionally to test his huge wings convinced those around him he could probably fly faster and farther now than any *two* wild ducks!

Boris, on the other hand, was upset with his slow healing process. Although his wing had healed and he could fly around the pen a bit, if he exercised too long he became tired. Some aching also reoccurred occasionally.

Still, Boris's overall prognosis was good and Mandrake was convinced when he and Boris were ready to leave the farm, they would leave together.

Late one night not long before Christmas when everyone was asleep in the shed there came a strange, soft scratching sound at the door, followed by a very light sniffing sound. But not the kind of sniffing sound Marvin made. Marvin's sniffing sound usually included some wet smacking of his lips, even a slobbering sound. But this sniffing sound was so low and so hesitating it could best be described as a kind of sneaky sniff—the kind of sneaky sniff somebody wants nobody else to hear. But Mandrake did!

"What's that?" he whispered to Boris as he peered hard into the darkness toward the loosely hinged door. Only a quarter moon was shining through a small window in the shed.

"I don't know," Boris said softly, "but don't make a sound or move a feather. Something's at the door."

Once again the sniffing and scratching sounds continued, then the hinges of the sagging door squeaked slightly. In another second, the door shifted and the sneaky intruder bounded in across the room in the moonlight. It crept in so swiftly, only Mandrake and Boris saw briefly what appeared to be a slinky furry animal with a large bushy tail. And when it attacked the chickens, pandemonium erupted in the shed.

"It's a fox!" Boris quacked loudly.

"EVERYBODY RUN FOR YOUR LIFE!" Delbert shouted as everyone scattered in all directions.

Once again Mandrake's courage surfaced. Ignoring any threat to his own life, he flew directly at the attacking fox with his sharp bill leading the assault. A whirling cloud of feathers, fur and straw filled the center of the room as the ducks and geese and chickens looked on in horror. When Mandrake hammered at the fox's head and eyes with his bill, the fox responded with grinding teeth and snapping jaws, accompanied by ferocious growling. Mandrake countered with his own high pitched, rapid-fire quacking, almost loud enough to break the fox's ear drums. And for a few brief moments, the contest between duck and fox was an even draw as everyone stared in disbelief.

Finally, when the battle registered with the ducks and geese, everyone jumped into the fracas to aid Mandrake—with Boris leading the troops. Quickly they encircled the angry fox with loud quacking, beating wings, and more jabbing with their razor-sharp bills.

The union of forces was too much for the bewildered fox. Overwhelmed with numbers, defeated in spirit and pained by the attacking flock, he broke loose from the circle of fire and made a bolt for the door.

As the sore and frustrated fox bounded over the hills into the darkness of the night, he reminded himself to skip this particular farm the next time he felt the urge for a fresh chicken dinner.

A few minutes after the near disaster in the chicken shed the farmer, his shotgun and Marvin came charging into the room. "What in tarnation's goin' on out here?" he demanded. Then he spotted some fur and feathers and a few drops of blood on the straw floor. "Hummm, looks like maybe it's that dang fox again! What do yah think, Marvin?" he asked turning to the bloodhound. "Sniff around boy an' see if yah can pick up his trail. Then we'll go get that buggar!"

Encouraged by his master, Marvin circled the room at full speed, sniffing here and there, scattering ducks and geese and chickens in all directions. Suddenly, near the door, he braked on all four paws. This action was immediately followed by a cocked head, then a deep, ear-piercing bay—a bay that surely might have been heard as far away as San Francisco Bay.

MANDRAKE FLEW DIRECTLY AT THE ATTACKING FOX WITH HIS SHARP
BILL LEADING THE ASSAULT

The farmer was impressed.

"What is it, boy? Yah got a whiff of him, didn't yah?" he said studying the edge of the door frame. "Hmm . . . more hairs and more blood—it's gotta be that dang fox all right!" He patted his dog's huge head. "Good boy, Marvin! Now we got his trail. An' it looks like he left in one heck of a hurry. Somethin' in here musta scared him pretty bad. Let's go get him, Marvin—LEAD THE WAY!"

As Marvin charged into the moonlight howling and baying, the farmer followed in hot pursuit with his shotgun and cries of encouragement. When their sounds had all but faded into the chilly night air, everybody gathered around Mandrake and thanked him for his bravery and courage. Mandrake was embarrassed by all of the attention.

Delbert was especially grateful to Mandrake for as we now know, foxes scared the daylights out of him.

But it was the old lead duck, Boris, who felt the greatest pride of all for he now knew the *next* most famous lead mallard duck of all stood before him.

12
It's Now or Never

Two days before Christmas the farmer came out to the pen and once again observed all of the ducks and geese more closely. As his eyes traveled the flock he stopped first at Mandrake and Boris, then moved on to the other ducks and geese. Apparently displeased with what he saw in the rest of his flock, he again turned his eyes back to Mandrake and Boris, this time focusing more intently on the two wild mallards. A slight smile crossed the farmer's face, followed by a silent nod of approval.

A major duck meeting was called that night in the shed long after the farmer, his wife and Marvin had gone to sleep.

Mandrake spoke first. "Boris and I must leave here tomorrow morning at dawn!" he said most emphatically. "If we don't, I have a very strong hunch the farmer is planning to serve wild duck for Christmas dinner!"

"I still don't know if I'm strong enough to make it to the Gulf," Boris said, "but I agree with Mandrake that it's now or never! So I'll give it my very best." The big drake stood tall, then threw back his chest and beat both his wings a few times. "My left wing feels almost normal," he said almost surprised.

"You sure look healthy to me," Delbert added encouragingly.

"And with Mandrake leading the way," Nathan said, "you guys will make it—I just know you will!"

All of the other ducks agreed that the two wild mallards had to leave early the following morning for their own safety. They had all grown very fond of Mandrake and Boris.

"Then it's settled!" Nathan said turning to Mandrake and Boris. "Now you guys have to get some rest. You still have a very long flight ahead of you."

To the east, the pink Christmas Eve dawn was beginning to break across the Midwestern sky as Mandrake and Boris, and all of the other ducks and geese, met outside in the center of the pen. The sun was still hidden behind the dark trees.

Boris cocked his big green head about, studying the sky all around. To the southwest, menacing storm clouds were beginning to form. And since the two ducks would be flying due south and storms usually travel west to east, Boris was concerned.

"I don't like the looks of that sky down there," he said disheartened. "That just might be a snowstorm brewing that could hit us later on. If it is, I'll have a tough time just keeping up with Mandrake, let alone fly through any foul weather."

Mandrake stretched up tall on his huge orange feet, then looked to the southwest. "I see it, too, Boris," he agreed. The young drake had noticed the shifting clouds and the darkening greys even before the old mallard did but did not want to alarm him. "Perhaps we can beat the storm south," he said, "or fly around it?"

"Well, we'll see . . . " Boris said. "I'll give you my best advice as we get closer, Mandrake, but remember, you're the lead duck now."

"I understand," Mandrake answered, "and we'll make it, Boris, I know we will!"

"Take care of this old fellow, will you Mandrake," Nathan said slapping a gentle wing on Mandrake's shoulder.

"And yourself, too, cousin!" Delbert grinned. "We know you've got it in you now and we're counting on you!"

"I'll do my very best cousins," Mandrake said smiling. "I love you guys, you know that, and we're both very grateful to you. You're a swell bunch of ducks."

"That goes for me, too!" Boris chimed in. "If it hadn't been for your kind hearts, I'd have frozen up there on that hilltop for sure!"

Then unexpectedly, a pretty young mallard hen from the back of the crowd of ducks came waddling up to Mandrake and gave him a big peck on the cheek. "You're my hero, Mandrake!" she said softly. "You saved all of us from that awful fox! We will remember you always." Then she stepped back into the crowd.

Following the young hen's lead, each of the ducks, and the geese too, thanked the big mallard drake for his courage and bravery. Many gave him a feathered handshake, others hugged him with their wings. All of the chickens clucked their gratefulness as well. It was a touching scene, one Mandrake would always remember.

But noise and excitement can often distract the memory. And that is exactly what happened when everyone was congratulating and saying good-bye to Mandrake and Boris on Christmas Eve morning. Everybody forgot about Marvin who had been asleep in his dog house near the front porch of the farm house.

With his natural protective instinct aroused and feeling a responsibility to the farmer and his wife to check out the ruckus, the bloodhound came barreling out to the pen with all four feet in high gear again. And to the surprise of everyone—and to Marvin's embarrassment—the big dog was wearing a new collar with ringing sleigh bells! A Christmas gift from the farmer's wife.

Still sleepy from the abrupt awakening, his weak eyes not yet adjusted to the predawn light and the nerve-shattering clanging of the collar bells, Marvin misjudged his speed and hit the pen gate full force! As could be expected from such a large galloping dog, the gate latch snapped open and Marvin suddenly found himself tumbling into the group of ducks—ringing sleigh bells and all!

Ducks and geese scattered in all directions! It was a noisy and alarming scene since the old dog had never before made such a terrorizing entrance. Even Mandrake and Boris were shocked and began to hop and jump short flights around the pen, not certain what would happen next. Then to add more fear to the escalating frenzy, Marvin began to chase the two wild mallards as though he had lost his senses!

But the wise old bloodhound had already recovered from his humiliating entrance and was in full control of the situation—in spite of his ear-piercing sleigh bells! "Don't worry!" he cried to Mandrake and Boris. "I'm not going to catch you, but I have to make it look good that I'm trying! The farmer will be out here any minute with his shotgun so you guys better high-tail it out of here right now!"

When Marvin got so close he appeared to almost bite a feather of Boris's tail, both wild mallards suddenly lifted off gracefully into the air, then circled overhead several times quacking their fond farewells and a Merry Christmas to everyone.

All of the ducks and geese below shouted back their best wishes for a safe flight and a very Merry Christmas too! Marvin also shouted a Merry Christmas in his deep base voice as well as shaking his head to add the ringing of his Christmas sleigh bells collar to the Christmas spirit.

Then the two ducks climbed higher and higher into the morning sky until they were only tiny specks on the pink horizon. When everyone turned their eyes back to each other to consider the new day, the farmer came running out with his shotgun.

"So what's all the commotion out here this time?" he asked loudly. "Is it that dang fox agin?"

While the farmer scratched his head in confusion and Marvin stared off into space, the flock of ducks and geese quacked softly, then marched past the farmer and Marvin into the shed.

It was at that moment that the farmer suddenly realized his flock of mallards was not complete. "Now where's them two big drakes I had ma eye on?" he asked himself. Then he remembered a serious oversight. "Dad blame it, Marvin! I fergot to clip the wings of all these buggars—should'a done it two weeks ago!" He looked at his dog. "Now we ain't gonna have duck fer Christmas, Marvin. The big ones is gone! Oh, well, I'll clip 'em later. C'mon on big fella, don't look so sad. Weren't your fault. We'll have us a good Christmas anyway. 'Member them steaks I put in the deep freeze? Well, how 'bout them? Sounds good, don't it?"

Marvin barked his approval. Then man and dog walked back toward the farm house.

With Mandrake leading the way the two wild mallards continued south, usually flying within sight of the Mississippi River. Although occasional strong

WITH HIS CHRISTMAS SLEIGH BELL COLLAR RINGING, MARVIN BEGAN
TO CHASE THE TWO MALLARDS AS THOUGH HE HAD LOST HIS SENSES

winds were encountered, harsh weather seemed unlikely at first. But later in
the day when the ducks were somewhere over northeastern Missouri, the winds
increased dramatically. Then the skies grew darker as ominous clouds slipped
in from the west.

"I was afraid of this!" Boris shouted to Mandrake. "We're headed right into
a snowstorm!"

"Can we fly farther east and stay head of it?" Mandrake asked.

"Won't work, my boy—storm's a big one an' coming in too fast! We'd be
blown hundreds of miles off course, I'd never make it! We've got to try climbing higher! It's our only chance unless we go down."

"THEN LET'S CLIMB!" Mandrake cried.

With Boris struggling to keep up, the two ducks flew higher and higher into the stormy dark sky. Turbulent clouds moved in below as the earth disappeared. Mandrake was getting concerned for the old mallard. "It's getting pretty dark down below," he said. "I can hardly see anything anymore!"

"I know!" Boris shouted. "But we've still got to go higher! I can't fly in this stuff much longer!"

As hard as they tried, the two mallards were unable to get above the snowstorm. Soon they found themselves in what seemed to be the very center of the blizzard. Seventy to eighty miles-an-hour winds were now tossing their fragile bodies about like corks on a raging sea.

Finally, Boris had had enough. "It's too rough up here for me, Mandrake! My wing is aching something awful—I've got to go down!"

Mandrake agreed, then began a steep dive down through the blinding snow. "FOLLOW ME, BORIS!" he shouted. "WE'LL FIND A SAFE PLACE TO LAND UNTIL THIS STORM'S OVER!" Down—down—down the two ducks dove. Faster and faster they dropped from the sky, their eyes and feathers filling with freezing snow—and still no sight of the ground below. Mandrake was certain any second he would crash headfirst into the very earth itself, with Boris piling in behind him.

Then instinct told the young drake he must pull up immediately. And none too soon! Just as he leveled off a large clump of tall trees frozen white appeared through the swirling snow dead ahead—not twenty feet away! He shifted into a steep climb, then hollered back. "PULL 'ER UP FAST, BORIS! THERE'S A BUNCH OF TALL TREES STRAIGHT AHEAD"

Boris swooped into a hard steep climb, straining his left wing to its limits. With only inches to spare, both ducks barely cleared the frozen trees.

At ground level the snow was still blowing hard and visibility was limited. Both ducks knew they needed a place to rest at once. After skimming along the tree tops and snow covered fields for a few miles, Mandrake spotted an old barn half buried in winter white. "Let's check it out first," he said to Boris. Dropping down the two ducks circled the barn looking for any signs of life inside.

"It looks like it's pretty deserted," Boris said.

"I think so," Mandrake answered, "and there's a hole at the top of the barn just under the roof eaves that should be large enough for us to drop through."

"Let's do it!" Boris said.

As soon as the ducks shot through the opening they folded their wings back, then tumbled down some soft hay, landing on the barn loft floor.

"Whew! That was a close call!" Mandrake said shaking off some wet snow.

"Hitting those frozen trees at the speed we were traveling down out of the sky would have been the end of us!" Boris said solemnly. "I'm sure glad you saw them!"

"Me, too!" Mandrake chuckled.

13
The Stool Pigeon

It was quite dark in the hay loft and it took Mandrake and Boris a few minutes to adjust their eyes. When they looked about, everything seemed quite normal but unusually quiet. The only sounds heard besides the blowing storm outside were a bunch of cooing pigeons on the roof rafters above.

"I don't hear any livestock down below," Boris said. "That would mean whoever owns this place must live somewhere else and keep their cows and horses there, too. Did you see any other farm buildings anywhere near when we flew in?"

"No," Mandrake said. "No farm house, no other farm buildings—just this barn."

"Well, that's normal sometimes. There's probably big hay fields under all this snow we just flew over and the barn's used only for storing hay."

"I'll make sure," Mandrake said. He leaned over a laddered opening to the floor below, then cocked his head from side to side, listening closely. "Nobody—nothing on the ground floor except a few pieces of farm machinery . . . a tractor, a wagon, stuff like that."

"Good! Then maybe we can get some peace and quiet and rest up here for awhile," Boris said. "By the looks of that storm outside, it could last for days." Then the old mallard reminded himself it was Christmas Eve. "Merry Christmas, Mandrake!" he said trying to grin with an aching wing. "I'm sorry you're not spending your first Christmas with your family."

"There's always next year," Mandrake said, "and there *will be* a next year!

Let's just be grateful we're still together and safe here in this loft. Merry Christmas, Boris! May we both have many more!"

"I suppose you're right, my boy, but we're still a long way from the Gulf and my wing's gotten stiff again, so I don't know if I can fl—" Boris was interrupted by a burst of loud cooing from some pigeons up above. He looked up disparagingly.

"Sometimes I think wild pigeons are luckier than wild ducks," he said. "They don't have to risk their lives migrating thousands of miles twice a year . . . farm pigeons live in barns like this year round . . . and city pigeons sit around on building ledges or statues and fly to the street or parks whenever they're hungry. Most people don't shoot pigeons—who wants to eat a pigeon, anywa—"

A darting figure from the rafters above dropped down, interrupting Boris's mournful speech. "Our lives, suh, are not as easy as you suggest!" a robust pigeon said in a thick southern drawl. He was obviously displeased with what he had just overheard. "Farm pigeons are often shot by farmers, some juss for the sport of it . . . city pigeons, like me, can be 'lectrocuted by high voltage lines, fall in tah roof fans, struck by cars and trucks . . . or freeze tah death on some of those ledges and statues you juss spoke of! An' there's neva enough for all us pigeons tah eat! So I ask you again, suh, do you really think we'a betta off than wild ducks like yourself?"

"Oh, excuse me!" Boris said apologetically. "I didn't know you could hear me up there on the rafters. I didn't really mean to belittle a pigeon's struggle to survive with humans. You've just shown me you have your problems, too! They're just different from us ducks. Forgive me! I was just feeling sorry for myself."

"Please don't take offense at what my friend Boris said, Mr. Pigeon," Mandrake pleaded. "He's very tired from being tossed about in this snowstorm with a sore wing. He was shot by a duck hunter not long ago and is still recuperating."

"And that's just part of the story," Boris countered. "We've been through a lot more than my gunshot wound. Why, if it hadn't been for Mandrake, here, I wouldn't be here at all!"

"No a'ffense taken, gentlemen," the pigeon replied in his southern drawl. I juss wanted tah set the record straight, that's all."

Mandrake had never heard a pigeon talk so slow, or so different. "Where are you from?" he asked.

"The name's Randolph Jefferson!" the pigeon said proudly, "and I'm from the beautiful port city of New Aw-lins, that's New Aw-lins, Lou-z-ana!"

"My name is Mandrake and this is my friend, Boris. We're from Canada."

"It's nice to make your acquaintance, gentlemen!" Randolph said nodding politely.

"What are you doing this far north?" Boris asked.

The pigeon glanced to the rafters above. "Visiting my yan-kee cousins for

"OUR LIVES, SUH, ARE NOT AS EASY AS YOU SUGGEST!" THE ROBUST PIGEON SAID IN A THICK SOUTHERN DRAWL..."

Christmas," he said. "And I presume you two are on your way south for the winter?"

"Yes we are!" Mandrake said, "and it's my first trip."

"MY—MY—MY!" the pigeon said somewhat surprised at Mandrake's large size. "You certainly don't look like a first-timer."

"He's been eating well on a farm in Iowa," Boris laughed, "but that's another story."

"What's your southern destination?" Randolph asked.

"Lake Pontchartrain," said Boris, "the Bonnet Carre Wildlife Management Area."

"Oh, good!" the pigeon said. "The lake's a beautiful place, as you probably already know, Boris. I often go there when I want to get out of the city for a few days . . . when I want to get away from the stress of my profession."

"Your profession? What do you do?" asked Boris.

"I'm a reporta . . . sorta . . . yah might say," Randolph said. "I gather tidbits of news here an' there, mostly local news around New Aw-lins, then report that news to a friend of mine who lives in an apartment high up over the city. His name is Aristotle—he's a parrot."

"Why tell a parrot?" Mandrake asked.

"Because Aristotle then tells his owna, a lady TV reporta, her name is Marla Falters." Randolph reflected on how Aristotle once described him. "I guess that kinda makes me a stool pigeon," he laughed.

"I KNOW WHO SHE IS!" Boris proclaimed. "I've seen her broadcast her TV show from Lake Pontchartrain on New Year's Day!"

"That's the lady!" the pigeon said.

"But how does Aristotle tell his owner?" Boris asked. "Parrots can't talk to humans."

Randolph seemed a bit upset with the question. "Of course not!" he said most emphatically. "But he *can* 'parrot' certain human words . . . and Marla is a very smart lady and very popular. That's why K-U-A-K TV has had her show on for years! That's "KUAK" TV for short!" Randolph joked, "in case you hadn't noticed."

"What's her TV show about?" Mandrake asked.

"Very important to us!" Boris interrupted. "Tell him about it, Randolph."

"It's a show about the annual migration of all of the birds and geese—even ducks," he winked, "that fly down from the north every fall to winter along the Gulf states—that all of us need to be aware of how some birds and geese and ducks struggle to survive alongside humans, that all such creatures need some protection if the public wants to continue to see and enjoy us."

"Look what happened to the late, great Labrador Duck," Boris reminded both.

"Exactly!" Randolph said. "That duck became extinct! But we're getting off the track . . . I'm a reporta, remember? What I want to know now is *your* story, gentlemen!"

Boris was eager to tell the pigeon how brave and courageous Mandrake had been since the two ducks' near tragedy on the Mississippi River. A true reporter at heart, Randolph Jefferson listened closely, then asked detailed questions for the best story.

When Boris had finished, the pigeon was deeply moved. "MY—MY—MY!" he said looking at Mandrake. "You, suh, are one brave mallard duck!"

"It was nothing more than any other duck would do under the same circumstances," Mandrake said modestly.

Boris ignored Mandrake's modesty and continued. "Have you ever heard of Mandrake I?" he asked the pigeon.

"Who hasn't?" Randolph answered. "Why I do declare there is not a bird along the Mississippi Flyway who has not heard of that super lead duck! And Marla knew him, too! In fact, she filmed him for her TV show on the lake a few years back . . . the last time he came down, as I now recall. She was very, very fond of that duck!"

"Well say hello to the grandson of that super duck!" Boris said pointing to Mandrake.

"I do believe, suh, you are putting me on!"

"No, I'm not!" Boris said proudly. "This *is* his grandson, Mandrake II!"

"WELL MY-MY-MY AGAIN!" the pigeon said looking at Mandrake. "Now I *do* see the resemblance." He turned to Boris. "No wonder this young drake has

90

so much spirit and courage—juss look at his heritage! Now you gentlemen must make the Gulf, ya hea! Marla will really be looking forward to it!"

Mandrake was embarrassed. He wanted to talk about anything but himself. "Where are you going from here, Mr. Jefferson?" he asked.

"When I finish visitin' with my cousins up above I'll stop and see some relatives in St. Louis for Christmas. Then it's on to New Aw-lins!"

"Not until the storm dies down, I hope," Boris said.

"I'm an excellent flyer, gentlemen, and when there is any break at all in the weather, I must continue on. And frankly, I can't wait to get home now and tell Aristotle who I juss met, and the rest of the story you juss told me."

"I wish you wouldn't do that, sir," Mandrake said.

"AND WHY NOT?" the pigeon asked surprised. "It's positive stories like yours that gives all us birds hope there may still be a future for us. It's heroic acts like yours, suh, that call the public's attention to our daily plight. We need more Mandrakes in this world, I do declare, or one day we'll all become extinct!"

"Mandrake is kind of shy when it comes to publicity, Randolph," Boris said. "He's had no experience with fame yet. So if you don't mind, we'd both appreciate it if you down-played this story to your friend."

"Okay," the pigeon agreed. "I don't want to embarrass anyone. I'll juss tell Aristotle there's another Mandrake coming down hea soon that's all!" (Of course it is important to remember here that Randolph Jefferson is a stool pigeon by his own admission.)

"That will be fine!" Boris said.

"So when are you gentlemen leaving for the Gulf?" Randolph asked.

"We're going to stay here for a few days," Mandrake said, "until Boris's wing improves."

"Good idea!" the pigeon said, "and I juss know you'll make it—you'll see!" He glanced to the rafters above. "Now I must get back to my cousins. Sure was nice meetin' you gentlemen . . . have a safe flight home from here on, ya hea!"

"It was nice meeting you, too, Randolph," Boris said.

"And that goes for me as well, Mr. Jefferson," Mandrake said. "I'm looking forward to seeing your beautiful lake Pontchartrain, Boris has told me so much about it. Maybe you'll fly over and see us when we get there?" The big drake looked at Boris, then back to the pigeon. "And we *will* get there—both of us!" he added.

"I surely will, Mandrake," the pigeon said most enthusiastically. "I would not miss your reception with Marla and your flock for the world!" Then with a flash of beating wings the pigeon darted to the rafters above, secretly and proudly convinced he had just heard a truly great wild duck survival story.

For the rest of the afternoon Mandrake and Boris filled themselves with hay seeds, then retired for the night. When they woke the following morning, the snowstorm had subsided some, but was far too intense yet for Boris to do any serious flying. They would have to wait.

The pigeon, however, had already gone south. But that was okay for Randolph Jefferson, for you'll remember he proclaimed with confidence he was an excellent flyer.

14
Remembering

Christmas day on lake Ponchartrain was very difficult for all of those who loved Mandrake and Boris. Most of the ducks were convinced Mandrake had given his life in an heroic but futile attempt to save their leader, Boris. Now everyone was sadly remembering how wonderful the two mallard drakes had been in life. If only they had been kinder to them, more understanding, more sympathetic . . . more loving. But it was too late now—or so they believed.

"Oh how we regret sometimes the things we should have and could have said when we were all together," one older duck said.

Martha seemed to take Mandrake's loss quite deeply, perhaps because the young drake had been hatched so small and insecure, last in line, and the weakest of all. While the mallard hen still had two other sons and a daughter, it was little Mandrake she had hoped and prayed would rise above his inadequacies and succeed in the wild duck world when others were certain he would fail.

Darrell, Mandrake's father, missed the little duck, too, but accepted his youngest son's fate as beyond his control. A wild duck's life is always full of risks, he reasoned to himself.

Boris, too, was very close to Martha and she missed him almost as much as her little son, for Boris had been the only other mallard in the entire flock that truly believed in Mandrake and what he could have accomplished if given the time.

Of course, sister Jenny had become closer and closer to her little brother, too, as the flock proceeded south. And by the time Mandrake had supposedly sacrificed himself for Boris, she knew Mandrake was the best brother she had. Now she missed him terribly.

But the one who suffered most and believed Mandrake was lost forever was Mandrake's sweetheart, Missy Prissy. The little hen was heartbroken and had great difficulty accepting the catastrophe that had just come crashing into her young life.

Later that night all of the ducks from Boris's flock held a Christmas homage for Boris and Mandrake at the edge of the lake. Forming a circle of touched wing tips, each duck stepped forward and expressed his or her admiration and respect for the two brave mallards.

Boris received a special tribute of gratitude for his faithful devotion to honor and duty as a lead duck, with the safety and protection of his flock always priority one. Also, Boris's deep understanding and patience when listening to any and all ducks who may have had personal concerns or complaints was recognized as a gifted talent. Everyone agreed Boris was the best lead duck they could ever remember, second only to his predecessor, Mandrake I. A praise Boris would have been proud to accept.

Lil' Manny, now referred to by all as Mandrake, was also recognized as the bravest of wild mallards in his self-sacrificing efforts to save Boris.

Any of the ducks who had made fun of or criticized the little duck in the past now stepped forward with their own sincere apologies and regrets. Even Ole' Mr. Duckworth admitted to everyone he had been "dead wrong about that little duck!"

Hector, too, was sorry for all of the mean things he had said and done to Mandrake, and now wished he could have apologized when Mandrake was alive.

Everett, the snow goose, was so moved by the eulogy he decided to make a short speech himself commemorating Mandrake—even though he hated talking to crowds. Stepping slowly out from the circle of ducks, he spoke softly but with pride. "If you folks will forgive a young and inexperienced goose for speaking, I'd like to say a few words about Mandrake . . . a mallard duck I had the brief privilege of knowing for such a short time."

All of the ducks were impressed and immediately gave Everett their full and absolute attention.

"I know I'm just an ordinary snow goose," Everett began, "and I'm not really a member of your duck family. But I want you all to know I feel both sad and happy inside tonight, sad that Mandrake is not among us, and happy just to have known such a fine mallard drake as Mandrake. He was, without a doubt, one of a kind!" Everett stopped short, holding back his emotions, then continued slowly. "And I feel very close to all of you ducks, too, now that I have experienced this tragedy with you. You are a fine bunch of ducks!" the snow goose concluded. Then he shied his head down and stepped back into the circle.

Deeply moved by Everett's special way of putting things, a loud roar of approval from all of the wild mallards echoed across the lake.

Ironically, the duck everyone least suspected would appreciate Everett's serious tribute to Mandrake was Hector. "As far as I'm concerned, Everett," Hector said, "you *are* part of our family! Your words of kindness about one whom you just met has shown each of us we all need to be more patient and understanding of each other . . . yes, and more loving, too!"

All of the ducks agreed and applauded vigorously.

"And personally speaking," Hector added grinning, "if it had not been for a hard lesson I learned from you and that punch you threw at me back on the river when I was still a young drake, I might still be a mean duck!"

Everyone laughed, then stepped up one by one and assured the snow goose he *was* part of this duck's family—now and always.

Holding back until last, Darrell, Darrell Junior and Aaron also expressed their regrets for not having recognized earlier Mandrake's courage and determination to succeed, even though the odds had been stacked against the little duck, initially. Now they openly admitted Mandrake had been one very brave duck!

15

On to Baton Rouge

For three more days following the departure of the pigeon, Randolph Jefferson, the snow and freezing wind continued to swirl around the old deserted barn. In the hay loft, Boris impatiently paced the floor, anxious to get on with the flight. But privately, Mandrake was grateful the winter storm had not subsided yet. He knew the old drake needed more time and rest to build his strength.

Finally, on the morning of the fourth day, a change in the weather.

Mandrake was the first to see the warming rays of the sun come shinning through the cracks of the old barn. Boris was still asleep. "Look!" Mandrake shouted, nudging Boris. "The sun's out!"

"Good!" Boris said. "It's about time!" He stood tall, swelled up his chest and beat his huge wings hard. "I feel much better," he said, "and my left wing seems almost normal."

"Then let's get out of here!" Mandrake cried excitedly. "Now how much farther is it to Lake Pontchartrain?" he asked.

"By my calculations when we landed here on Christmas Eve we were probably a little north of Hannibal, Missouri—that's on the Mississippi River but we couldn't see the river or the town in the snow storm. So if I'm right, we've still got some seven hundred miles or more to the Gulf. If my wing doesn't go bad on me again, we should make it there in two . . . three days."

"So what are we waiting for?" Mandrake asked. "Let's go!"

Both mallards lifted off the hay loft floor to the hole at the roof peak, then sailed out into a bright blue sky. A crisp blanket of snow covered the earth below. It was a great day for flying.

For the first two days everything was fine with both ducks. In fact, Boris was flying with so much renewed energy, he sometimes darted up and down in the sky to try and convince Mandrake he had completely recovered. But Mandrake was taking no chances with the old drake and insisted they make frequent rest stops to feed on the Mississippi—often to the dismay of Boris.

Then on the third day out, just after the ducks had finished feeding on the river, Boris became exhausted once again, this time more seriously, much to his own surprise. One minute he had been flying like the young drake Mandrake was, the next minute he was losing altitude—and fast!

Mandrake looked back at the faltering Boris. This old mallard has just got to make it to the Gulf with me, he told himself. Then he can rest and heal properly. "I know you're tired, Boris," he shouted. "Let's go down—NOW!"

"But we just took off from the river not an hour ago!" Boris cried, "and we're not even to Memphis, Tennessee yet!" Again the old mallard took a serious dip in the air.

"I DON'T CARE-WE'RE GOING DOWN!" Mandrake shouted. Then he peeled off and dove for the ground. As it was the lead duck's decision, Boris followed without question.

As the ducks pulled out from their dive, an old country filling station appeared at the side of a cracked and crumbling two-lane road. A rusty old Ford truck with a rope-tied canvas roof sat in front of the station pointed south. That's good! Mandrake told himself. An old road like this means fewer travelers so we have less of a chance of being seen—or shot!

Beneath the sagging roof of the gas station two men were talking as one reached into his back pocket for his wallet. After paying his bill, he climbed into the old Ford and fired the engine. With some coughing and sputtering, the truck pulled onto the road, then slowly picked up speed.

"HERE'S OUR CHANCE, BORIS!" Mandrake shouted. "FOLLOW ME—WE'RE GOING TO FLY RIGHT INTO THE BACK OF THAT OLD TRUCK . . . UNDER THE CANVAS TOP!"

"BUT—BUT WHY?" Boris asked. "IT'S CRAZY!"

"FOLLOW ME!" MANDRAKE SHOUTED TO BORIS. "WE'RE GOING TO FLY
INTO THE BACK OF THAT TRUCK, RIGHT UNDER THAT CANVAS!"

"NOT IF WE'RE GOING TO MAKE THE GULF!" Mandrake cried. "WE HAVE
TO KEEP GOING, AND THERE'S NO PLACE TO HIDE OUT AROUND HERE!"
"LEAD THE WAY!" Boris shouted.
When the gas station attendant saw the two ducks appear overhead, then
zoom into the back of the old Ford as it rumbled down the road he mused
to himself, "By golly! Them's two smart mallard ducks . . . hitchin' a ride in
the back of that old Ford sure beats flappin' your wings all the way to the
Gulf. I speck that's where they're headin' now that winter's closin' in up north."

Scratching his head beneath his worn cap, the attendant walked back into his station.

Under the stretched canvas in the back of the old Ford Mandrake and Boris found a wonderful surprise—a whole truck load of golden eared corn! More corn than any two ducks could eat in a year! Immediately they began to eat their fill as the old truck rattled on.

"This is weird!" Boris chuckled. "Two wild mallard ducks, *riding* south in the back of a truck! We're supposed to *fly!*" The old drake could not help but feel a little embarrassed, if not ridiculous. But he was very glad he was riding now. His wing was acting up again and he wondered if he would be able to fly much farther anyway, whenever the truck stopped? And he prayed that was still a long way off.

"Just try and relax . . . and enjoy the ride," Mandrake told Boris. Then he paused, considering their next move. "We are going the right way, aren't we Boris?" he asked.

Boris stuck his head out the back of the truck and checked the position of the sun. "Yes, my boy," he said. "Okay so far."

Then he saw the humor in it all. "Just don't tell anybody we *rode* part way to the Gulf in this truck. No one would believe us anyway," he chuckled. With plenty to eat and free transportation, so far, the two mallards settled back for a bumpy, rattling ride, surprised, yet somewhat amused that a wild duck's life can be so simple and fun at times, and so life-threatening at other times.

For most of the day the two ducks feasted on eared corn and stared out the back of the truck. Only an occasional small country town appeared at the side of the road, at which time the driver would slow, but never stop—thank goodness!

But when the sky began to shift to deep purples to accept the nightfall, the driver suddenly veered his truck off the road once more, this time stopping at a country gas station with a small cafe next door. "Fill 'er up!" he said to the gas attendant, then headed for the cafe.

"This may be the end of the ride for us," Boris groaned sadly. "My wing's stiff as a board so if anyone looks in here, I want you to take off as fast as you can, Mandrake. Save yourself!"

"Shhh!" Mandrake whispered. "Don't make a single quack. It's not over yet!"

Moments later a young boy came out of the station and walked up to the man pumping gas into the truck. "What's in the back of the old Ford, Dad?" he asked curiously.

"Don't know, son. Haven't looked."

"Kin I look?"

"Sure! Go ahead, son. Jess don't touch nothin,'" his father said as he continued to squeeze the gas pump handle.

Mandrake knew Boris needed more rest and would not be able to fly very far if they had to leave the truck. But he was not about to desert the old mallard. Now he needed a plan of action—and fast! Then an idea struck him. Boris had called the next move whether he knew it or not when he said his wing was 'stiff as a board.' "Play dead!" Mandrake whispered to Boris. "Lay back on the corn stiff as a board!"

"Play what?" Boris asked dumbfounded.

"Do it now!" Mandrake repeated. "The boy's headed this way to take a look. Put a glassy stare in your eyes—play dead—and don't move a single feather!"

Boris followed his lead duck's orders immediately, and none too soon. Seconds later the young boy stepped up onto the back bumper with one foot. Peering inside the truck, he seemed disappointed. "There's jess a bunch a' eared corn in here, Dad," he hollered back, " . . . an' a couple a' dead ducks! Guess the driver's been up on the river doin' some huntin' since duck season's here." He climbed down and returned to his father. "They look like they'd be mighty good eatin' too," he said to his father. "Theyz really *big* ducks!"

The father ignored his son's secret wish. "You're jess hungry, son," he said, "'cause it's 'bout supper time. Why don't you go into the cafe an' have your mother fix you a bite. Then you can man the pumps fer a spell while I get me somethin.'"

The boy passed the truck driver coming back from the cafe.

"My tank full yet?" the truck driver asked the boy's father. "Got to get to Baton Rouge 'fore sun up."

"She's full now!" the boy's father said capping the tank. "But you didn't eat nothin' that fast, did yah?"

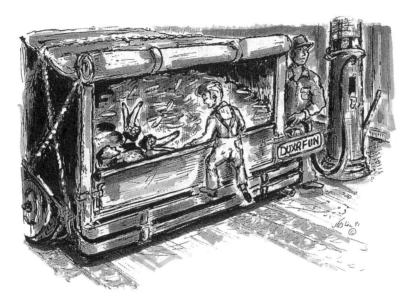

"THERE'S JUST A BUNCH A CORN IN HERE, DAD!" THE BOY
HOLLERED BACK, "AN' A COUPLE A' DEAD DUCKS!"

"Naw, just coffee. Don't have time."

After paying for the gas, the truck driver checked the right front tire which
seemed a little bald. But two hard kicks convinced him the tire would last
until Baton Rouge. Then he crossed in front of his truck and checked the
left front. That one looked a lot better. Satisfied, he climbed back into his
cab and fired the engine once again, then directed the old truck onto the
country road. Not once did he walk around the back of his truck. The stow-
aways were still safe.

"Huh!" the boy's father muttered a bit disgusted as the truck disappeared
into the darkness. "Reckon he's savin' up his appetite fer them two big ducks
he's got in the back . . . oh, well, 'least he got a full tank a gas."

Lulled to sleep by the old Ford's vibrating groans and a hypnotizing, almost
full moon, Mandrake and Boris caught a few more winks. Then, precisely at
the stroke of twelve midnight as the rattling truck chugged its way through a
small Louisiana town sirens rang, bells clanged and horns tooted—then, daz-

zling fireworks of red and silver and blue and green burst across the dark sky turning night into day with explosive fury!

"WHAT'S ALL THAT?" Mandrake cried peering out the back of the truck.

Boris could not help but laugh at Mandrake's alarm. "That, my boy, is the beginning of a New Year! It's a celebration to bring in the New Year . . . and it happens every year, all over the country exactly at twelve midnight on December thirty-first. That's when everyone hollers 'Happy New Year' to everyone else, so Happy New Year to you, Mandrake!"

"WOW!" Mandrake exclaimed. "My first New Year! Happy New Year to you too, Boris! Now we *must* get home today for sure!"

"Well, we'll give it our best shot, Mandrake," Boris said, "but keep your feathers crossed."

"We'll make it, Boris, you'll see!"

An hour or so later as the old Ford chugged its way through the night, the air suddenly turned warm and humid, as if someone had waved a magic wand welcoming the two ducks to the deep south.

Boris was feeling much better now, his aching wing had all but disappeared and he was very glad to be away from the harsh winters of the north, and happier still that he and Mandrake were so close to home. Yet, he knew only too well there was one more risk, one more crisis to navigate before it was all over.

Suddenly the truck slowed, shifted down, then left the old road and climbed up onto a main highway. Heavy traffic appeared at once. Cars with high-powered engines and whining tires accelerated around the truck, their flashing headlamps reflecting off the shiny green heads of the two mallards. Mandrake was in awe at all of the speeding traffic.

"I'll bet we're a funny sight to these drivers," he laughed. "Two live wild mallards sitting on a load of corn in the back of this truck watching everybody rush to nowhere."

Boris did not answer. He was getting worried now. All of this traffic meant only one thing—Baton Rouge was close, and bail-out time for the two ducks was about to begin! Now the question was, would they be able to escape from the truck without getting caught? And would he be able to fly, or must Mandrake go on alone?

As the sun began to light the morning sky with streaks of lavenders and pinks, the old Ford shifted down again, this time pulling off the busy highway and onto a deserted side street. After winding through an industrial area for a few blocks, the truck driver carefully eased his truck up to a tall grain elevator, switched off his lights and cut his engine.

Both ducks jumped up onto the steel end-gate, poised to take-off.

As the driver approached the back of his truck, Mandrake quacked loudly to Boris, "LETS FLY!" And *fly* they did!

Taken totally by surprise, the truck driver jumped back in awe as the two big mallard drakes shot past him in a gush of whistling wind, then climbed speedily into the breaking dawn. "WHAT'S THIS?" he muttered aloud, "WILD DUCKS IN THE BACK OF MY TRUCK? CAN'T BE! I'M SEEIN' THINGS!" But before he could regain his composure, the two ducks had already disappeared into the brilliance of the rising sun.

At long last Mandrake and Boris were on the final leg of their perilous journey, a harrowing adventure only a wild duck could experience.

16
Everett Meets Edith

On New Year's Eve, when Mandrake and Boris were riding south in the back of the old Ford truck, Martha, Missy, Jenny and Everett were all very sad as they swam aimlessly around Lake Pontchartrain. None of them had the slightest idea, of course, that Mandrake and Boris were still very much alive.

But in spite of Everett's despondency over Mandrake, the snow goose did have a turn of good luck, much to his surprise. Swimming off by himself into some thick reeds at a secluded part of the lake, a strange and wonderful thing happened; something that would change the young snow goose's life forever.

"HONK! HONK! HONK!" came a loud sound from deep back in the reeds.

Everett swam closer to investigate. Once again the sound repeated itself, this time even louder! "HONK! HONK! HONK!"

Fascinated and curious, Everett swam deeper into the tall grass, straining his long neck forward and cocking his head from side to side. Again, more honking! "Well, I'll be darned," he muttered, "Guess I'm just gonna have to swim in here farther and see what's makin' all this honkin'! Whatever it is, it ain't comin' out—that's for sure!"

Lowering his long neck and head to glide beneath the low hanging grass, Everett propelled himself deep into a darker part of the watery thicket. Once inside, the puzzle was solved!

Floating quietly on the water with her long white neck turned down in a gracious bow was the most beautiful young snow goose Everett had ever seen! And when she batted her eyes at him affectionately, Everett was dumbfounded.

"Hello!" the lovely goose said. "My name is Edith. What's yours?"

"Uh-Uh-Uh," Everett stammered, trying desperately to find his voice. "My name is Ev-Ev-Everrrrr-ret!" There! He got it out—finally! "And I'm a snow goose," he snapped confidentally.

"I can see that, silly!" Edith laughed. "So am I!"

"That's right . . . so you are! I can see that, too, madam—I mean, mam—I mean Edith!" Everett was babbling now, so excited and embarrassed that he did not know what to say next. So he said nothing.

Aware of Everett's shyness, Edith took control of the situation, smart young goose that she was. "Are you from Canada, Everett?" she asked. "I am, my family and I, that is. They're all on the other side of the lake today. We just flew in a few weeks ago."

"Yes, mam—I mean Edith! I'm from way up in Can-e-da near the Arc-tic!"

"Is your family and your flock here with you?" Edith asked coyly. The young snow goose liked Everett a lot and she wanted to find out if he had found a mate yet.

"Nope! Came down here alone," Everett answered quickly. Then he thought about what he had just said. "Well . . . I'm really not alone. I got two brothers, I think, down here somewhere probably . . . and I got a whole bunch of wild mallards I know. I flew in with them. They're very kind and considerate ducks and they kind of adopted me, for which I am very grateful." His heart was pounding so fast now he could hardly control himself. She was just too beautiful!

"That's nice," Edith said. "Then you have both family and friends here on the lake."

"Well, you know what they say: 'Birds of a feather must stick together!'" Boy! That was a pretty dumb thing to say to her, Everett told himself.

But Edith did not think it was dumb at all. "That's as it should be," she said. "Geese like to be together just like ducks. I think it makes us feel safer in groups. Of course there are exceptions at times . . . like me today. I flew over here just to be alone for awhile. And I'm really glad I came over today," she added.

"Me, too!" Everett blurted out. Then he surprised himself again. "You sure are a pretty snow goose!"

"HELLO!" THE LOVELY GOOSE SAID, "MY NAME IS EDITH! WHAT'S YOURS?"
"UH-UH-UH," EVERETT STAMMERED, TRYING DESPERATELY TO FIND HIS
VOICE.

"Why thank you, Everett! I think you are cute, too!"

"Aw, shucks!" he replied. "I'm just a plain ole' snow goose."

"You underestimate yourself, Everett. I know you are a kind and sympathetic snow goose—it shows. And I'm certain that's why the mallards took
you in as their friend." She swam closer, then nuzzled her soft white head
against Everett's cheek. "Do you have a girl friend?" she asked brazenly.

"Nope!" Everett said. Then an uncontrollable instinct arose. "Do you—do you have a boy friend?"

"Not yet!" Edith answered quickly—"that is, unless you want to be my boy friend."

"WOW-OH-WOWEEEEEE-WOW!" Everett shouted. He began to swim wildly in circles, flapping his huge wings hard against the water.

"Is that a 'YES'?" Edith laughed.

"YES SIR!—I MEAN, YES MAM!—I MEAN YES—YES-YES I WOULD—I MEAN I WILL!" Everett babbled. Then he let out a series of loud honks as he continued swimming in circles, this time splashing Edith with sprays of water. "HONK! HONK! HONK! HONK!"

Edith sat quietly on the water, watching her new boy friend express his happiness and love for her. She was just as thrilled as Everett, of course. Just a little bit more controlled, that's all.

When Everett finally calmed down and accepted his new love as real, the two snow geese swam out of the reeds side by side and into a wonderful new life together.

But alas! Everett thought to himself. If only Mandrake had lived to meet my new love. Then everything would have been perfect. But who knows? he reflected. Maybe, just maybe Mandrake, and Boris too, are still alive—somewhere?

As Everett and Edith swam together around Lake Pontchartrain on New Year's Eve, Randolph Jefferson was landing on Aristotle's window ledge, twenty stories above New Orleans. Reporter Marla Falters always left her parrot's cage open during the day to allow him the freedom to fly about her apartment. At dusk, Aristotle would always return to his cage whether Marla was home or not.

"Come to the window!" the pigeon shouted to the parrot. "I've got a real scoop for you this time!"

"What is it?" Aristotle asked gliding down to the window screen.

"I got the best story eva," exclaimed Randolph, " . . . 'bout two wild mallard drakes flyin' down hea from the north. 'Course they'a not hea yet, but they will be, you can count on them!"

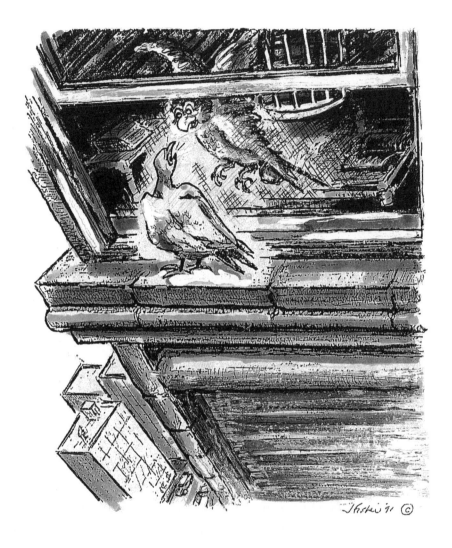

"COME TO THE WINDOW!" THE PIGEON SHOUTED TO THE PARROT.
"I'VE GOT A REAL SCOOP FOR YOU!"
"WHAT IS IT?" ARISTOTLE ASKED GLIDING DOWN TO THE WINDOW
SCREEN.

"So what's so unusual about ducks flying down here from the north?" Aristotle asked. "Tens of thousands of them do it every year."

"I know that!" Randolph snapped. "But this story is different—totally! And it's a real surprise. Are you ready to listen?"

"Try me!" the parrot said.

"Well, we have to go back to Canada this last spring where this little duck was hatched . . ." Randolph began. Then he related the entire story as told to him by the two wild mallards, and how they ultimately survived a flight in which ordinary wild ducks would surely have perished—"at least they were both alive when I last saw them in a barn hay loft near Hannibal, Missouri," Randolph concluded.

The parrot was flabbergasted. "And you're positive this little duck is Mandrake II, the grandson of Mandrake I?" he asked wide-eyed.

"Absolutely positively!" the pigeon said. "He looks *just* like him!"

"Boy! That is one fantastic story!" Aristotle said. "I sure hope they make it down here by tomorrow morning. I know Ms. Marla would be thrilled. She loved Mandrake I, you know, and filmed him many times on her TV show at the lake."

"I know!" Randolph said. "That's why I'm telling you this story. Somehow, you have to let her know Mandrake II is on his way right now as we speak."

"I'll think of a way," the parrot said. "Count on it!"

"Good! Now I must be off," the pigeon said. "I've got to check on a few things before going over to the lake tomorrow morning. I'll let you know if everything comes off as we've planned." With that, Randolph darted off into the sky and disappeared behind some tall buildings.

Aristotle paced back and forth along the window sill, thinking hard of how he would tell Marla the good news. Then the idea struck him.

17
The Reunion

The New Year's Eve traffic in New Orleans was building in the streets below when reporter Marla Falters turned the key and burst into her twentieth floor apartment. It was already 10:25 p.m. Aristotle was sitting in his cage in the dark when she snapped on the lights.

"Hi, baby!" Marla said happily. "How's my pet parrot tonight? Did you have a good day? I hope so! Mine was exhausting. I had to work late at the station tonight to prepare for my TV show in the morning." She kicked off her shoes and walked to the parrot's cage.

"HELLO, MARLA—HELLO, MARLA—HELLO, MARLA!" Aristotle said in rapid fire.

Reporter Falters laughed. She was glad to be home, snug in her little apartment high above the noisy streets below. "You make me feel so good, baby," she said. "Sometimes I wish I could tell you all about my day and you could tell me all about yours." She checked the parrot's food and water. "I just know you have secrets. Know how I know? Because you are just about the smartest parrot in the whole world! That's how I know!"

Aristotle blinked his eyes in agreement.

Marla laughed again. "I know it's New Year's Eve but I think I'll stay home with you tonight. I need my rest to be fresh tomorrow when we film all of the beautiful birds on the lake that fly down here every year to spend the winter." She thought about her job and the show's purpose. "Somebody has to let everybody else know that some of these winged creatures are in danger of extinction if we don't protect them. That's why Lake Pontchartrain is also a bird refuge." She yawned, shaking her head. "But now I have to lie down, I'm really tired." She dropped into her sofa and quickly fell into a light sleep. Aristotle saw his chance.

"MANDRAKE IS COMING! MANDRAKE IS COMING! MANDRAKE-THE-SECOND IS COMING!" he chanted.

Reporter Falters shook her head, then blinked her eyes open. "What did you say, Aristotle, Mandrake-the-Second? There is no Mandrake-the-Second!"

"MANDRAKE-THE-SECOND IS COMING—HE'S COMING—HE'S COMING!" repeated the parrot.

"But there is *no* Mandrake-the-Second!" Marla said emphatically.

Again Aristotle repeated himself.

"There was only *one* Mandrake!" Marla insisted, ". . . and he's gone! He was a wonderful wild mallard but he's gone, Aristotle—gone forever! Now let's both get some sleep." She covered the parrot's cage, then retired to her bedroom.

As Marla drifted off she began to review in her mind what her parrot had repeated so insistently. "What did that silly Aristotle mean," she whispered to herself, "when he said 'Mandrake-the-Second is coming?' Did he mean *Mandrake* is coming back? That's impossible! I haven't seen Mandrake in over three years! Golly, this is crazy," she thought, "listening to my parrot as though he knows something I don't. This is dumb. I've got to get some sleep right now!"

In a few minutes, Marla was asleep, dreaming about birds and geese and herons and cranes and ducks, and more ducks, then mallards . . . and then . . . Mandrake, that wise and handsome mallard drake she had named herself when she first saw him on the lake years ago . . . that wonderful duck she had grown so very fond of and missed ever since.

"HELLO AGAIN FROM LAKE PONTCHARTIAN, LADIES AND GENTLEMEN . . . AND KIDS OF ALL AGES! AND HAPPY NEW YEAR TO EVERYONE!" Marla smiled as the cameras rolled. "This is your reporter, Marla Falters, coming to you once again live from the edge of Lake Pontchartrain on station K-U-A-K TV, Channel 52, your local television station. You're witnessing here on your television screen the ninth annual documented bird migration of many of the birds, geese and ducks and other beautiful winged creatures that fly down from · the north to winter here with us on the Gulf. Some of these birds have flown thousands of miles to be with us from as far away as the cold Arctic, just to enjoy our mild winter climate . . . and for the protection of wildlife sanctuaries like our Bonnet Carre Wildlife Management Area here.

"And by the looks of everybody swimming or flying around or standing here on this warm grassy bank quacking or chatting contently, it looks as if they are all very happy to be here . . . and of course we're happy they're here, too!"

As reporter Falters continued with her show, Martha, Missy and Jenny left the lake edge and climbed up onto the bank near the reporter to see what the human commotion was all about. Everett and Edith soon followed them onto the bank, then Missus Missy Prissy, and finally, Hector.

Most of the rest of Boris's flock were diving and bobbing for food near the shoreline, including Mandrake's father, Darrell, and his two brothers, Darrell Junior and Aaron. Such a large congregation of wild ducks, along with other water fowl and birds delighted reporter Falters who was anxious to show on television as many different species of birds as possible.

Overhead, Randolph Jefferson was observing the entire annual TV production which he hoped would soon be transformed into Marla's best show ever!

As reporter Falters continued to talk to her TV audience off camera, her cameraman panned the ducks and geese along the bank of the lake. Then he turned his camera out across the open water for the TV audience to view a panoramic picture of the beautiful lake scene.

More curious than anything, Missy turned her head to follow the cameraman's line of sight. "Look, Martha!" she cried, ". . . over the water just above the horizon to the northwest!"

"What is it, Missy?" Martha asked spinning about.

"There are two big mallard drakes headed this way," Missy answered.

"Oh, my goodness, could it be?" Martha exclaimed excitedly.

"Could it be *what?*" Missy asked raising her voice. She watched Martha strain her neck, then cock her head to get a better look at the fast approaching mallards.

Then the mother hen quacked loudly to get everyone's attention. "LOOK UP THERE, EVERYONE!" she shouted ". . . TO THE NORTHWEST JUST OVER THE LAKE . . . THERE ARE TWO BIG MALLARD DRAKES FLYING IN!"

"Who is it?" Ole' Mr. Duckworth grumbled from the shoreline.

"I see them!" Hector said. "Two big mallards, sooooo?"

Darrell and Darrell Junior and Aaron looked up from the water's edge briefly but were too busy bobbing for food to be bothered with Martha's excitement.

"I bet *I* know who they are!" Everett exclaimed. He was grinning like a silly goose now.

Missy held her breath in anticipation.

Jenny was stunned into silence.

And Martha cried, overjoyed, "IT'S MANDRAKE AND BORIS . . . IT'S MY BOY—MY BOY! OH MY, OH MY, OH MY! AND HE'S ALL GROWN UP SO BIG AND STRONG!"

"Oh, Martha," Missy sobbed openly, "are you sure—*really* sure?"

"I'd know my boy anywhere!" Martha said proudly. "He's the bigger one, the one in the lead . . . and that's Boris just behind him. They're both safe!"

"I just knew if any duck could rescue Boris it would be Mandrake," Everett proclaimed proudly.

Jenny looked up, thrilled as the two big drakes flew in closer and closer. "IT IS MANDRAKE!" she cried, "AND BORIS IS RIGHT BEHIND HIM!"

"Well, if it *is* Mandrake," Hector said, "he sure has grown up big—wow!"

All of the ducks on the bank and near the water's edge were watching intently now as the two big ducks came skimming in just over the lake, not five hundred feet from the shoreline.

Recognizing the mallards as Mandrake and Boris, Darrell and Darrell Junior and Aaron decided to wade ashore and greet them. Even though they had shown little interest in Lil' Manny's survival in the past, now they realized they had underestimated Mandrake and wanted to tell him they were sorry—and proud of him, too!

"OH, MANDRAKE!" Missy cried. "IT REALLY IS YOU!"

"Isn't he beautiful, Mother," Jenny said. "Isn't he the biggest and most handsome mallard drake you have ever seen? My baby brother . . . all grown up!"

"Yes, dear, he is beautiful," Martha smiled. "And I just knew if he had the chance, he would grow up big and strong one day, and now—here he is! Oh, thank goodness he's safe at last!"

As the quacking and clamoring of the ducks grew louder and louder, the cameraman turned to Marla. "Why are all these mallards so excited watching two more fly in? What's going on?"

Of course we all know now reporter Falters had a nose for news and was a strong advocate for the protection of bird wildlife. Her highly rated New Year's Day television show from Lake Pontchartrain welcoming all such bird life from the far north was clear evidence the public was equally concerned. However, the fact that Marla had not yet related Aristotle's parroting to what was about to happen is of little importance. After all, her logic had been sound. She knew in her heart Mandrake was never coming back. And the thought of another Mandrake would be wishful thinking—if not a miracle.

What does matter now is that reporter Falters knew something wonderful was about to take place in the lives of these magnificent mallards—just what, she wasn't sure, but she would soon find out.

"I DON'T KNOW WHAT'S HAPPENING!" she shouted to her cameraman as she ran toward the flock of ducks, ". . . BUT FOLLOW ME!"

Mandrake and Boris splashed down very near the edge of the lake, not twenty feet from the ducks and Marla. Then they swam quickly to shore and climbed up onto the grassy bank amidst a roar of thunderous quacking from all of Boris's flock.

Reporter Falters stared hard at the big lead duck—she could hardly believe her eyes! The big mallard drake was, without a doubt, a dead-ringer for the first Mandrake, with huge orange feet, bright emerald head and a long yellow bill.

This is almost unbelievable, she told herself—another Mandrake? Yet, here he is standing before me! How wonderful! Now I know what Aristotle was trying to tell me last night. How he knew about this new Mandrake I'll probably never know . . . but I do know I have one smart pet parrot.

Almost as excited as all of the ducks around her, Marla moved quickly among the flock, studying their reaction to the two big drakes that had just landed. Of course she did not understand exactly what all of the ducks were quacking so excitedly about, nor the reason for all of the warm wing hugs and affectionate pecks Mandrake and Boris both received—or did she?

18
Change of Command

Now for all of you who have not yet learned how to communicate with ducks, I will do my best to translate what actually took place on the shore of Lake Pontchartrain after Mandrake and Boris climbed from the water and joined the excited mallards.

First off, all of the ducks congratulated Mandrake for his courage and bravery and for saving Boris's life.

Then Boris related the two ducks' entire harrowing experience, while Mandrake listened with bowed head most of the time. Boris began with the time he was shot on the Mississippi River and Mandrake dove to his rescue, to the very end of the long and hazardous journey when both ducks flew from the back of the old Ford truck to freedom. The old mallard also held up his left wing—the splintered bone still visible but now healed—for all to see and examine. Then he continued.

"I would like to say here and now that had it not been for this very brave and courageous young drake standing before us, I would not be here today." Boris then offered a quick wing tip salute to Mandrake. "I'm sure you all know that but I had to say it.

"Now it is obvious from what I have just told you that Mandrake has become one of the smartest and bravest mallard ducks I have ever had the privilege of flying with. He has the vision and the wisdom to solve life-threatening situations on the spot, to analyze any crisis and figure a way out—if there is any at all! He is protective, understanding . . . and sympathetic of others, beyond question. And most of all Mandrake will put his own life on the line for others without hesitation. He is the most unselfish duck I have ever known!

"Notwithstanding all of these excellent character traits, Mandrake is also a skillful navigator. He now knows the route of the great Mississippi Flyway—and its pitfalls and hazards—probably better than most of you here today will ever know!" Boris paused, studying the crowd of ducks. Then went on.

"Now you all remember that before we left the cold north I told you to pick a new lead duck for our return flight next spring, that I was going to retire then and fly off the wing of your new leader. Well, I've decided to advance that schedule. I am announcing my full retirement right here and now!" All of the ducks leaned forward in anticipation. "So we need to pick a new lead duck, right? Of course we all know lead ducks are first nominated, then seconded and then voted on by all of you—and only a majority vote picks the winner. Now I'm going to speed up this whole democratic process," Boris continued, "by nominating Mandrake II as your new lead duck. If anyone else chooses to nominate any other duck, please speak up now." All of the ducks remained silent. Nary another duck's name was mentioned. Mandrake, too, remained silent, the southern sun now reflecting brightly on his glorious plumage. "Then we need a second," Boris said calmly.

To the astonishment of almost all the ducks, an unsuspecting voice was heard from the crowd, loud and clear: "I SECOND THE NOMINATION!" Hector cried. "LONG LIVE MANDRAKE II . . . OUR NEW AND HEROIC LEAD DUCK!"

Immediately, a unanimous roar of approval was heard from the ducks with cheers and best wishes quacked by all, as reporter Falters looked on fascinated with excitement.

It should be pointed out here that Mandrake had not the slightest inclination Boris would nominate him for the new lead duck of Boris's flock. It was a total and delightful surprise to the young drake, but a position he willingly accepted with choked pride.

Now at last, Lil' Manny, the scrawny little duck who always believed he could win in a wild duck's world if he tried hard enough and long enough, was officially elected lead duck of his own mallard flock.

Boris was the first to shake Mandrake's wing, then all of the other ducks moved in one-by-one and congratulated him.

"You'll make a great lead duck, Mandrake," Boris said amidst the uproar of the ducks, and I'm very proud to have recommended you for the job."

"I'll do my very best," Mandrake said—then, talking aside to Boris and Martha, "but I want to thank you and Mother the most. Both of you had faith in me when some were not so sure. It was your faith and your love and encouragement that kept me going."

"That's nice of you to say, my boy," Boris said, "but it was your own self-belief and determination that made you the duck you are today. You never gave up, no matter how tough things got, regardless of the odds. We're all very proud of you, Mandrake."

"Yes, we surely are, son," his mother said.

"Me, too, little brother . . . oh, excuse me." Jenny laughed. "I guess I should say *big* brother now!"

"You were wonderful, Mandrake," Missy said giving him a big hug.

"And that goes for me, too!" Everett said patting his dear new friend on the shoulder. Then he pulled his lovely snow goose mate close and introduced Edith. Mandrake was very pleased that Everett had found love so soon.

Missus Missy Prissy waited her turn, then congratulated Mandrake and told the big drake how happy she was that he and Missy could now start a new life together.

Finally, Mandrake's father, Darrell, and his two brothers, Darrell Junior and Aaron stepped forward somewhat sheepishly. "We were wrong about you, son," Darrell said, "and the boys and I want to apologize for our bad behavior in the past. All three of us are proud as the dickens of you, Mandrake, aren't we boys!"

"Yes we are!" Mandrake's two brothers repeated one after the other. "And we're sorry the way we treated you."

"There's nothing to forgive," Mandrake said giving them all a big hug. "It's in the past."

Reporter Falters was too excited to remain silent any longer. "Something wonderful has just happened here!" she told her TV audience. "I can feel it, and I think I know what it is. For those of you who were watching our television show a few years ago you may remember a handsome wild mallard drake we introduced to you as Mandrake. He led his flock of wild mallards to and from our lake every year for years. In fact, when he was no longer with us, many of you wrote or called asking, 'Whatever happened to Mandrake?'"

Now I am happy to report we have a *new* Mandrake whom we'll call Mandrake II because he looks so much like our first Mandrake, they *must* be related! And I'm certain we're going to see a lot more of this beautiful drake in the future because the way his loved ones are hoovering around him, I think he's just been elected the new lead duck of this mallard flock. Isn't that fantastic!"

Smiling brightly, reporter Falters moved in closer to the big drake with her mike and camera. "Welcome to Lake Pontchartrain, Mandrake II," she said. "We're all so happy to meet you. Would you please say 'hello' to the people of New Orleans?"

How reporter Falters actually knew what had just taken place among the flock of wild mallards we can only guess. We did suggest earlier the reporter had a nose for news and a love for wild birds, particularly ducks. But maybe, just maybe, reporter Falters had also learned how to communicate with ducks . . . as your writer did . . . but just never told anyone?

Mandrake, too, must have sensed Marla Falters's love for ducks and was eager to express his views on "live" television, explaining how really neat wild ducks are. When the cameraman panned in close, the big mallard drake quacked incessantly for almost two full minutes while reporter Falters, Martha and Missy, and the rest of the flock beamed with pride.

THE END

WHEN THE CAMERA PANNED IN ON MANDRAKE, THE WILD MALLARD
QUACKED INCESSANTLY FOR ALMOST TWO FULL MINUTES—WHILE
REPORTER FALTERS AND MARTHA AND MISSY AND EVERYONE BEAMED
WITH PRIDE.